AUTHOR JULIA BAILEY has wo
and lived in a leprosy colony o
scariest thing she has ever don
Redland, Bristol. They live in a
one Rose Cox grows up in. So far none of them have managed to
time travel.

Julia E Riley

To R and L who know who they are. To I for the Year.

Published in paperback by SilverWood Books 2010

www.silverwoodbooks.co.uk

Copyright © Julia Bailey 2010

The right of Julia Bailey to be identified as the author of this work

has been asserted by her in accordance with the Copyright,

Designs and Patents Act 1988.

All rights reserved. No part of this publication may be reproduced,

stored in a retrieval system, or transmitted in any form or by any means,

electronic, mechanical, photocopying, recording or otherwise,

without prior permission of the copyright holder.

ISBN 978-1-906236-35-9

British Library Cataloguing in Publication Data

A CIP catalogue record for this book is available from the British Library

Set in 11pt Garamond Pro by SilverWood Books

Printed in England on paper from sustainable sources

TIME WISH

Julia Bailey

SilverWood

Chapter One

Cossins Place – Leading To Chandos Road

The day that Rose Cox travelled in time began in a very ordinary way.

She had breakfast with her mother in the gloomy, half-light of their dining room. Dark mahogany furniture towered over them and long velvet curtains were pulled tight against any speck of sunlight. As they said grace, Rose fiddled with the tassels on the lace tablecloth and sighed to herself.

I really must try to be good today, she thought. I've been awfully rude and sulky recently, particularly towards Mama. I know – I shall try to get through the whole day without committing a single sin!

Their vicar, the Reverend Sylvester of St Saviours, preached terrifying sermons about sinners who led disastrous lives and suffered even worse deaths. He would lean out of his pulpit, eyes bulging and long, lanky arms waving accusingly down at his congregation: "Guard your mortal souls against *sin* as the hand of *death* is ever ready to *strike*!"

The number of sins you could commit seemed endless to Rose, and today at breakfast things did not go well. To start with she experienced:

Greed – asking for the last slice of buttered muffin.

Envy – of her mother, who having forbidden Rose the extra portion went on to eat it herself.

Anger – at her mother for eating the muffin.

Rudeness – sticking her tongue out at her mother.

Lying – denying she had stuck it out.

Disobedience – slamming the door when she was sent up to her room, after her mother had especially asked her not to.

And finally:

Vanity – stopping halfway up the stairs to admire her new hair ribbons in the mirror.

By this time she had lost count. She was obviously overflowing with sin and her only hope was to make up for it by being really good when she was older. Perhaps she could become a missionary in darkest Africa? She would spend her whole life saving souls and living in mud huts. She would finally die of some terrible tropical disease: probably involving black spots and her toes dropping off. At this point her mother – very old by then, but somehow able to make the long trek through the jungle – would appear by her bedside and cry:

"If only I had let her have that last piece of muffin!"

Up in her room Rose sat on her bed and swung her legs. Her mother was a lot older than other children's and she'd always been rather strict, but since they moved house she seemed to be angry all the time.

Rose stared around her room, feeling bored, as she often did.

She didn't like her room – it was too green. Green striped wallpaper; green silk counterpane; bottle-green curtains; even cold, green linoleum covering her floor. All chosen by her mother, of course.

When I grow up, Rose promised herself, in *my* house, I'll have pink candy–stripes and sherbet yellow, no green anywhere!

Rose strummed her fingers along the rails of her iron bedstead. One knob was missing where she'd unscrewed it and thrown it out the window in a fit of temper. Then she got up and wandered round the bedroom, running her hand over her dressing table, wardrobe and chair. Apart from these her room was quite bare. Her mother had made her leave her collection of china dolls behind in their old house. She had told Rose that, now she was eleven, she was far too old to play with them. Only one book was allowed in her room – her Confirmation Bible. Rose had to read a page each night before she went to bed.

She had just two pictures on her walls, her mother's choice not hers. One showed the Queen surrounded by all nine of her children. This was Rose's favourite; she loved the idea of large families with lots of brothers and sisters to play with. She did feel sorry for Queen Victoria though, she was *so* sad at losing her husband. But at least she had all those children and lots of palaces and castles to live in.

The other picture always made Rose shiver and she tried not to look at it, particularly at night, when it was dark and she was alone in her room. It was in black and white and showed a tall man in a long robe standing on the edge of a cliff. His eyes seemed to be blazing with anger. In one hand he held up a Bible and in the other he dangled a terrified child over the side of a deep ravine.

Written along the bottom in curly black letters it said: *Repent Ye Oh Sinner!*

Rose heard the grandfather clock in the hall chime nine. That meant she'd been up in her room an hour and it should be time for lessons. She went out onto the landing and hung over the banisters, her long black hair falling down into the stairwell. She was three flights up, but by tipping herself upside down she could see right into the entrance hall. Janetta, their maid, was pulling on her gloves as she chatted to Cook about the day's shopping.

"Rose Cox!"

Rose had failed to notice her mother standing on the landing below. Mrs Cox stared up at Rose accusingly. "It is *most* unbecoming for a lady to lean over banisters like that – and extremely impolite to listen to others' conversation."

"I'm *so* sorry, Mama." Rose tried unsuccessfully to sound as though she really meant it.

Mrs Cox put a hand up to her forehead and sighed heavily. "Your atrocious behaviour at breakfast has given me one of my sick headaches – I hope you are thoroughly ashamed of yourself for causing me such distress! I shall have to lie down this morning and we will do your school work this afternoon instead. *Please* try to be quiet whilst I am resting, Rose." She frowned up at her daughter, looking severe in her black, taffeta dress with its high buttoned collar. She'd worn nothing but black since Rose's father died last year. Then, with another deep sigh, she swept round and disappeared into her darkened bedroom.

Rose felt guilty for causing her mother's migraine, but she was also secretly relieved that she wouldn't have to endure their morning lessons. Her mother had been teaching Rose herself, since they could no longer afford a governess, and it wasn't going well.

Rose decided to practise some dance steps on the landing. When they'd lived in the big house in Clifton she'd had dancing lessons with her cousins and it had been one of her favourite things to do.

She started with some twirls and jumps using her pillow as a partner, but after only a few minutes her mother flung open her bedroom door and glared up at her. "Rose! It sounds like a herd of elephants crashing on the ceiling. Please show some consideration. You know I am feeling unwell today."

At that moment Janetta, their maid, appeared with a wicker basket over her arm. "I could take her out shopping with me, Ma'am. I'm just going down Chandos Road."

Rose could see her mother was reluctant to say yes. She thought their local row of shops were 'horribly common' compared to the sophisticated malls of Clifton. But on the other hand, Mrs Cox was desperate for some peace and quiet.

"All right, Janetta. On this occasion I will allow it. Rose, you must wear your hat and gloves at all times and no running in the street or talking to the shopkeepers –except to say 'please' or 'thank you'. Is that understood?'

"Yes, Mama!"

Rose gave a quiet whoop of excitement. She wasn't often allowed to go out shopping so this was an unexpected treat.

The early summer sun was warm on Rose's face as she stepped out into the wide road, but she knew she wouldn't be allowed to remove one bit of her heavy outdoor clothing, no matter how hot she got. Large, stone and brick-fronted houses lined the dusty street; over half of them were boarded up and unsold. Rose tried not to look at these, they reminded her of her father and how he'd lost his fortune building them. She liked looking at the ones where families *had* moved in: with striped awnings over their front doors and flower – filled gardens. A black and white sign stood at the corner of the street, the paint almost as shiny and new as the day Rose's father had placed it there. Rose liked to stop and run her hands over the raised letters: *Cossins Place – Leading to Chandos Road.*

Rose loved Chandos Road. It was lined on either side with busy little shops, selling everything you could possibly need. Janetta hurried her on past the chemist, the ironmonger, the dress-maker, the wet fish shop and then at last Rose's favourite of all – the wool shop. The outside was painted a dark blue and above the door were stone carvings of a red bird, a moon and a five-pointed shape that Rose knew to be a pentangle. A small porch way led into the shop: it had black and white floor tiles and frosted glass panels on either side. Engraved on these panels were the words: *Experienced Attention* and *Personal Service.*

Once inside the shop it took a while for her eyes to adjust to the darkness. There was no lighting apart from some glowing coals in a small, iron fireplace right at the back of the shop. Then, as Rose's eyes got used to the gloom, she could make out the outline of a figure, hunched to one side of the fire, rocking and knitting, knitting and rocking.

The inside of the shop was covered in wool, stacked from floor to ceiling, every colour and thickness imaginable. There were little, round-topped tables scattered about the room, each one covered with knitted items – socks, bonnets, scarves, gloves and tiny, perfect baby clothes that both Janetta and Rose loved to coo over. Some of them would have fitted Rose's china dolls – if only her mother had let her keep them.

The figure by the fire smiled over at Rose. 'Vat arr you kneeting now, leetle Rosebud?'

She was knitting and rocking so fast she was almost a blur but Rose could just make out her wrinkled, brown skin and dusty, black dress and cape. A lace veil covered her face, but underneath you could tell she was smiling. She always smiled at Rose.

'You arr *so* serious, Rose, you must be happee more!'

But Rose found it difficult to smile to order. People were always telling her to 'Cheer up, it might never happen!' But in her experience very little did ever happen and she often wished it would.

'I'm still knitting that scarf,' she admitted. 'I do try to do three inches a day, but somehow I always get called away to do something just as I'm getting started.'

'Neverr mind, Rosebud, neverr mind.' Mrs F smiled and rocked, and rocked and smiled.

Nobody knew what the 'F' stood for or where Mrs F came from.

'Why don't you just ask her?' Rose demanded, when Janetta and cook were gossiping about it yet again.

'Because that would be very rude and personal,' Janetta had replied, looking shocked.

So it remained a mystery.

Rose ran her hands down the racks of needles and stroked the soft skeins of rainbow-coloured wool. When I grow up I'll have a place like this, all of my very own, she promised herself. I'll sit in the rocking chair and poke the fire as much as I want – and nobody will be able to tell me off!

Janetta had gone to sit in the high-backed chair opposite Mrs F. Without a word the old woman reached up and took a clear, glass ball from the mantelpiece and placed it on the table between them. Janetta glanced nervously over at Rose; she knew Mrs Cox disapproved of the old lady and her fortune telling. Would Rose tell on her? Surely not? After all, she had always been far kinder to Rose than her mother ever was. To her relief the little girl seemed absorbed in a stack of knitting patterns and didn't even glance over at them.

Janetta shouldn't have been so easily fooled. Rose might look as though she was engrossed in *Bonnets for Baby*, but she was an expert at listening in on adult conversations.

Janetta turned back to Mrs F. 'Just a quick reading, if you can. I mustn't be late back or the mistress will have my guts for garters! I'm particularly interested in this afternoon, Mrs F. Can you be that specific?'

The old lady arched an eyebrow. 'Not usually, but on this occasion I think I see something for you...'

Mrs F pushed back her veil revealing her eyes, two black pools of ink that reflected no light, not even the flickering of the flames in the grate. She passed her hands several times over the crystal ball, took a deep breath and closed her eyes. The shop was silent except for the crackle of the fire and the rustle of Janetta's skirts as she shifted nervously in her chair.

Mrs F wrinkled up her forehead, looking puzzled. 'I'm getting the sign of a magician, can that be right?'

Janetta looked surprised, then her face lit up. 'Mr Tricks! Mr Ernest Tricks is my, well, my...' She blushed furiously, once again glancing nervously over at Rose and lowered her voice. 'My, er – young man, Mrs F. We're attending a talk together on the African Missions this afternoon – if all goes well. Can you see any more about it?'

The old woman passed her hands over the ball once more. Her face broke into a smile and she nodded at Janetta. 'There will be a few minor obstacles to overcome, but I see a happy ending to the afternoon. Although...' Her forehead creased again and her face darkened. She looked over at Rose. 'I need to do a reading for the young lady. *She* seems to play an important part in this story.'

Janetta looked alarmed, but Rose had whisked around and was already on her way over to them. 'Please, *please*, Janetta, I won't tell Mama. I promise. Please!'

Janetta struggled with her conscience, but her desire to find out how her date with Mr Tricks would go got the better of her and she moved aside to let Rose sit opposite Mrs F.

Once again, the old lady closed her eyes and passed her hands over the crystal ball. Rose felt a strange fluttering sensation in her stomach, as if hundreds of butterflies were hammering their wings against her insides. For a moment everything seemed to go very dark, then very light. She had a strange whooshing noise in her ears and a feeling of falling backwards very fast. She could see pinpoints of light like stars, which then merged together to form the outline of an old woman. It was Mrs F leaning anxiously towards her – or was it? It was the old lady's face but her clothes were different and

15

the shop looked different too. It was much brighter, the little tables had disappeared… and where was Janetta?

'I am so sorry little one, but I had to see if you could do it. I had to try, for your sake – and for the others.'

From outside the bright windows a steady hum came and went and Rose could see the blurred outlines of strange shapes and colours. Mrs F took her hands.

'You are in terrible danger, Rose. I need you to do something that will take all your courage and willpower.'

Rose was shaking. She was already sick with fear. How could she promise to be brave?

Mrs F's hands were warm and dry and held hers in a firm grip. 'I *will* take care of you little Rose. You must trust in me, as I trust in you. I know you are brave and you are clever. I believe that when the time comes you will know the right thing to do, and you will find the strength to do it.'

Rose nodded her head. Partly because she was scared and thought that if she did Mrs F would let her go home, and partly because she had been waiting all her life for something like this to happen.

Chapter Two

In the Wool Shop

'What do you want me to do?' Rose stared over at the old woman. It was odd to see her in this harsh new light, odd too, to see her face without the lace veil shielding it. She looked much younger, her face less lined, but her eyes still black as coals.

'I cannot tell you everything now, Rose. We haven't much time before you must be back. Certain events will happen today, which will make things much clearer to you. You must concentrate hard on everything you see and hear, and at the end of the day you must make a choice. It may be a hard choice... it may mean leaving everything you know and love. Do you think you can do this little Rose?'

'Yes!' Rose was surprised how easily the answer came.

Mrs F smiled at her, the corners of her eyelids crinkling with pleasure. 'Good, Rose, very good! But there is something more.' Her smile disappeared, her face became deadly serious. 'It is not just yourself who is in danger. I will help you to escape, but you in your turn must help someone else – even if it means making another hard decision to leave a place and person you love.'

This time it took Rose much longer to answer. In a small voice, she whispered, 'Yes.'

From outside the window, she heard a strange thumping music and a high pitched ringing sound that kept stopping and starting again. But inside the room all was quiet except for the crackling of the fire, its flames dancing in the glass sphere, which still lay between them.

Mrs F stood up. She took a poker, red hot from the coals, held it high in the air and then brought it slamming down onto the crystal ball – shattering it into four jagged pieces. She handed one to Rose.

'Keep it safe, little one. When the time comes, hold it tight and wish. Wish very, very hard.'

Rose nodded, her heart beating furiously. She took the broken piece and placed it in the pocket of her coat. It felt heavy there, much heavier than you would expect from such a small piece of glass.

Mrs F sat down and put her hands over the remaining three shards of crystal. 'Close your eyes Rose. We're going back and sometimes that can be even harder.'

Rose clenched her eyes shut, feeling relieved. She wanted to go back now. The shop that was the same and yet not the same, the weird noises outside the window, the way Mrs F had got younger and lost her foreign accent – it all made her feel queasy and confused. The tumbling sensation started again, but this time much worse. Her head felt as if it was being squeezed, tighter and tighter, in a giant vice. Terrified, she opened her eyes. A kaleidoscope of colours spun in front of her. She opened her mouth to scream then everything went black.

She couldn't tell how long it stayed like that. It seemed both to last forever and be over in a split second. A face gradually swam into focus above her – it was Janetta. Rose burst into tears and then, to the maid's astonishment, threw her arms around her.

'Come along, Miss Rose. The fresh air'll make you feel better. It was just a little turn, that's all.'

They were back out on the street. Janetta had rushed her out of the wool shop, after apologising to Mrs F for the 'disturbance' Rose had caused. Rose barely had time for a backward glance at the familiar figure by the fire, but it was just long enough to catch the old lady smiling at her – and then, she wasn't sure, but did Mrs F point her knitting needle towards Rose's coat pocket?

Her mind was racing. What had really happened in the wool shop? Had it all been a dream when she passed out? She'd fainted once before – the day her father died. They'd taken her in to see his body: he was lying in his best suit on her parents' bed. His skin was the wrong colour, like the grey putty the workman used round the windows in the new houses. The room was full of relatives, all stuffed into the overheated room, all muttering about money.

'Foolish venture!'

'Ruined!'

'Lost his fortune and left poor Anne on the wrong side of Whiteladies Road – and with practically no servants!'

Rose had felt a boiling rage start to churn inside her. Nobody cared about her darling Papa! Nobody cared that he'd died! Why were they all saying such horrid things about him? She thought it was wonderful that he'd built a whole street of houses. It wasn't his fault nobody bought them. It made her feel special to live in a house built by her own father, and she hadn't minded leaving the big house in Clifton at all. She liked being part of the brand new district of Redland; she loved watching the builders scrambling over their rickety scaffolds, pushing the streets of Bristol farther and farther out into the countryside.

Her great aunts huddled round the bed like crows in their black mourning clothes. 'His death's a blessing in disguise – at least his life insurance will pay off the worst of their debts.'

Rose's head had begun to spin. How *dare* they say that about Papa! It suddenly hit her in a great wave of despair: she would never see him again, never hear his voice calling, 'Rosebud, where's my Rosebud?' They'd never go for rides round the Downs in their pony and trap, both of them singing away at the top of their lungs. She'd felt sick and hot and cold all at the same time. The last thing she'd heard before she slumped to the floor was her mother's voice: 'Oh, how unnecessary! Trust the child to embarrass me, today of all days! Janetta, please remove her.'

Janetta hurried Rose along Chandos Road. She was eager to get the shopping done so she could get back in time to iron her best dress and coat. She wanted to make sure she looked her best for Mr Tricks.

Rose was still puzzling about the wool shop. When she'd fainted at her father's bedside she didn't remember having any strange dreams. Also, everything that had happened in the wool shop with Mrs F was quite clear in her mind – not at all muddled like dreams normally are when you try and remember them. She thrust her hand into the scratchy wool of her pocket. Yes, it was definitely there. She could trace the sharp edges of the broken glass and feel its weight against her hand. If it really *had* all happened and if it really *were* all true, then she must keep her promise. It would be sinful not to. Or was it sinful to have made a promise to a fortune teller? Rose wondered what Reverend Sylvester would have to say about it all.

No, she thought to herself, a promise is a promise. I must do what Mrs F asked. I'll see what happens today and then at bedtime I'll try to work out what the right thing is to do. After all, she did say I was in terrible danger and maybe she's a kind of angel, sent down from heaven to help me. Maybe Papa sent her.

Janetta was examining her shopping list: 'Potatoes, cabbage and beetroot. We need to visit Mr Guppy's for those.

Mr Guppy, the greengrocer, had a magnificent moustache which he waxed into two long points that stuck out a good six inches either side of his face. Rose always had an overwhelming urge to reach up and pull them very hard. Luckily Mr Guppy was completely unaware of this. He beamed down at Rose, slipping an apple into her hand when Janetta wasn't looking. Rose had to hide it in her pocket to eat later – she'd been told many times that eating in the street was 'horribly common'.

Next stop was Yeo Bros, the butcher's, which reeked of sawdust and blood. This morning they'd gone in to buy a joint of beef. Rose tried to hold her breath so she wouldn't have to smell the raw meat. One time she'd wandered over to the back of the shop and looked through to the large room behind, where rows of legless carcasses were hung up on vicious-looking hooks, their blood dripping red stains onto the yellow sawdust. She screwed up her nose at the memory and stared fixedly at the floor.

Janetta looked down at her. 'Why are you pulling that face Missy? If you don't watch out, the wind'll change and you'll be left like that!'

The younger Mr Yeo was grimly wrapping up their meat in greaseproof paper. Despite their jolly boaters with the red ribbons, neither of the Yeo's ever smiled. As he handed over the package, he nodded towards Rose. 'You'll have heard about the outbreak then? Three little 'uns on Brighton and two on Cowper Road's gone down with the diphtheria. One of them's really poorly I've heard.'

Janetta looked anxious.

'I hadn't, how awful! It spreads like the plague in those houses – they're built far too close together. And there's Mrs Dando with eleven kiddies in one house. I hope its not one of hers has it?'

Mr Yeo shook his head glumly. 'God works in mysterious ways. Ours is not to question why. Good day!' He turned round and smashed a meat cleaver into a leg of lamb.

Once safely out of the butchers they crossed over to the dairy. This was another of Rose's favourite places. She loved the cool, tiled shop front with its sweet smell of fresh milk. She liked to hold the little milk pails with their tightly fitting lids. But best of all were the stalls at the back of the shop where the cattle came in to be milked. In each stall there was a large brass ring, and above every ring a wooden block with the cow's name on it. Rose knew them all off by heart: Bluebell, Star, Gertrude, Emily, Bessie, Trixie, Daisy and Buttercup.

The cows munched the grass up on Redland Green and twice

a day, they swayed down the hill: a long line of mooing, shuffling cattle, passing down Cossins Place, on their way to Chandos Road for milking.

'Honestly, it's like living in a farmyard!' Mrs Cox would moan. 'If only we had the milk delivered in carts like we did in Clifton. It really is *too* much having to see the dirty beasts.'

But Rose loved the cows. Sometimes she would get up at dawn, throw up her window and gaze down at their wide, dappled backs, breaking through the early morning mist.

Janetta pushed open the door to the dairy and Rose noticed at once that the eldest Perkins boy, Aubrey, was already in there. Rose's mother considered the Perkins family to be, 'just dreadful! They don't attend a proper church, they let their children run wild in the streets, *and* I've heard Mr Perkins has some most peculiar habits.'

This last remark had driven Rose mad with curiosity, but her mother had buttoned up her lips disapprovingly and refused to say more. However Rose had overheard Cook talking to Janetta about a cold plunge bath that Mr Perkins had had built in the cellar at Number 34 Cossins Place.

'And they all go in it see, every morning. Says it's for their health, mind.' At this point Cook had lowered her voice so Rose could barely hear the next bit, but she was pretty certain it contained the words 'stark naked'.

After this, whenever Rose bumped into Aubrey she couldn't help herself thinking about his morning plunge. When she saw him playing out in the street, he wore a brown wool coat and knickerbockers, usually with several rips in the knees. But in her mind's eye, she would see him leaping into the cellar pool, his body shimmering pink and white like a fish. The thought made her cringe with shame and embarrassment every time it popped into her head. This was quite a problem as Aubrey seemed to go out of his way to seek her out and chat to her. Today was no exception.

'Hello there, Rose. Mr Bartlett let me milk the cows today. He said I wasn't half bad for a beginner. 'Course he wouldn't let you do it 'cos you're a girl.'

That annoyed Rose enough to overcome her embarrassment. 'Well actually, *dairy maids* are girls and they get to milk cows all the time. Anyway you can't have been that good – you've got milk splashed all over your boots!'

Aubrey grinned. 'By Jove! So I have. Are you coming to the park later? I've got some of those new rollerskates and I'm going to try them out – or is your mother still fearfully strict with you?'

Rose scowled. She knew her mother was difficult, but she didn't like other people to criticise her. Of *course* she wanted to go to the park and of *course* she wanted to see the rollerskates: she'd seen pictures of them in her Sunday magazine and they looked *so* much fun. But of course he was right – her mother would never allow her to go.

'No thank you – I'm busy,' she said coolly, turning away. Janetta had finished ordering the milk and was standing, waiting for her by the door.

Aubrey grinned again, the freckles on his nose wrinkling up. 'See you later alligator!'

As Rose trudged back up the street towards her house, she couldn't help thinking about the long hours of boredom stretching ahead of her. What on earth could she do to fill the time – read the Bible, sew, perhaps some knitting? Rose had no idea that the afternoon wasn't going to be boring at all and what happened in the next few hours would change her life forever.

It was early evening. The clouds were softening from blue to pink in the patch of sky outside Rose's window. Thoughts were tumbling and racing through her mind and she gripped the window ledge, trying to slow them down and make sense of them all. Pictures from the afternoon flashed through her mind. She saw a boy in brown knickerbockers, his arms outstretched like a seagull, swooping around a small patch of wasteland on his skates. She saw his pale face and dark hair. Then his hands clutching at his throat as he doubled over. In her head she heard Mrs Fs voice: 'A hard choice'... 'Leave everything you know'... 'Terrible danger'... 'Wish very hard.'

A harsh knocking came from the hall below, much louder than normal, and she heard the sound of Janetta's feet running towards the front door. Quickly Rose crept out onto the landing and leaned over; she couldn't see the caller's face but she recognised the voice – it was Sarah, governess to the five Perkins boys. The conversation was urgent, but too muffled for Rose to make out what they were saying.

As Janetta turned to come back in, cook walked out of the kitchen, her hands floury from bread making, Rose could just catch Janetta's voice: 'Poor little boy. Poor, poor little mite!'

Then Cook threw her apron up over her head and sobbed.

The sound of Cook's crying brought Mrs Cox out of her sitting room and, after more hushed discussions, she sent Janetta to fetch

Dr Ormorod. His black hat and case brought back memories of his visits when her father was dying, and made Rose shudder. He and Mrs Cox talked in the sitting room for what seemed to Rose like an eternity. Nobody took any notice of Rose. Eventually she came and sat quite openly on the stairs and no one told her off. Not even her mother, when she finally came out of her room and ushered the doctor out of the house.

'Rose, something very sad has happened. Eustace Perkins has died of diphtheria. It was very sudden and let us pray he didn't suffer too much.' Mrs Cox dabbed her eye with her handkerchief. 'Apparently he became quite delirious at the end and kept calling for his mother, even though she was right there beside him. Poor little child, he was only three years-old... but at least his parents have the comfort of the other four boys to sustain them.' Mrs Cox gave a dramatic sigh and brought her hand up to her forehead. 'Although Janetta tells me the oldest child – what is his name? Oh yes, Aubrey – they do give their children such ridiculous names! Well, Aubrey has been complaining of a sore throat this evening and Dr Ormorod tells me this is one of the first signs.'

Rose felt her stomach contract and a wave of sickness hit her. She had often seen Eustace, a jolly, fair-haired little chap, running along with Aubrey to the park or the shops. She couldn't believe he could be dead so quickly. And now Aubrey was ill. Would he die too?

Her mother carried on mournfully, 'Dr Ormorod says the next stage is often fatal. The disease turns your whole throat grey, then it closes it right up and you die from slow suffocation – a truly terrible end!' Mrs Cox dabbed at her forehead again. 'Rose, I must ask you this, it's very important for me to know – have you had any contact with the Perkins children? I do hope you have not, as you are well aware that I disapprove of the way they are brought up. Their parents are far too affectionate with them. I wouldn't be surprised if that's how the boys caught the diphtheria – all that kissing and spoiling.'

Rose felt the hallway start to spin, just like when she'd seen her father's dead body. She heard her mother asking if she was all right, then everything went black.

When she came to, she was lying on the chaise-long in her mother's sitting room and Janetta was dabbing her forehead with lavender water. Her mother's harsh voice was issuing instructions: 'Take her up to her room, Janetta. Honestly that child is far too sensitive for her own good! It's not as if she really knew the boys. When I talked to Dr Ormorod he recommended gargling with Dr Collis's tonic water. Can you see if there's any in the medicine cabinet? Maybe I should send Rose away for a few weeks by the sea, till this dreadful epidemic passes…'

Rose still felt groggy from her faint, but she knew she couldn't tell her mother what had really happened that afternoon, she just couldn't! She had committed a terrible sin and this must be God's punishment. Maybe she was going to die too?

She'd seen the row of little gravestones in the churchyard at St Saviours – carved with tiny cherubs and heartbreaking inscriptions:

Our dear angel taken for a sunbeam
A little lamb gathered unto His flock

She didn't want to be one of those children, sealed in a small white coffin, carried by black horses with nodding plumes to lie in the cold, dark, suffocating earth for ever and ever. She wanted to grow up and travel the world, she wanted to have her own wool shop, she wanted to live in a big house crammed full of children. She didn't want to die yet!

Rose lay in bed after Janetta had tucked her up with a glass of warm milk and her favourite ginger nut biscuits. She couldn't sleep. A bright new moon lit up her room, and outside her window the wind moaned and the branches of the old copper beech threw eerie shadows against her curtains.

Rose closed her eyes and tried again to make sense of the events of the day. Mrs F had said that everything would become clear to her and she could then make a choice – a choice to help her escape from terrible danger. Well she knew the danger now. She knew she might have caught diphtheria, she knew she might die from it like poor Eustace. She also knew she had to wish hard and hold the crystal – but what should she wish for? The old lady had said the choice meant leaving everything she knew and loved… Rose looked around her bare room and thought, briefly, of her mother. The person I loved most in the world is already dead, she thought, there is nothing left here that I really love.

She picked up the broken glass and closed her eyes. From the landing below she could hear a muffled sobbing sound. It was her mother, crying.

I can't do it, I just can't! Rose lay back down. It was probably all nonsense anyway – or witchcraft, which was worse. She curled herself up into a ball and tried desperately to fall asleep.

From outside her window came a heavy creaking noise, and then the sound of branches raking and scratching along the panes of glass. Rose's eyes snapped open. A shaft of moonlight fell on the jagged shard of crystal, turning its surface into a million dancing points of light. At that moment Rose knew what she must do – for herself and for Aubrey. She mustn't be scared any more.

Rose leant forward, grasped the shattered glass and this time she wished. She wished very, very hard.

CHAPTER THREE

The Thin House

When Rose woke up the next morning she could tell without opening her eyes that the storm of last night had passed. The air outside was calm and there were no branches scratching at the window pane. There was a strange humming noise that seemed to get louder and softer by turns; she thought she'd heard it somewhere before but couldn't remember where. She opened her eyes and then immediately shut them again. She waited ten seconds and then reopened them. The room was very bright, the walls a shocking pink colour. It was not her room.

Slowly she turned her head to look out of the window. It was covered by a garish blind, also pink, but printed with huge dolls with enormous eyes – eyes that appeared to be staring straight at her. A sudden blast of noise filled the room… screams, moans and a deafening drumming.

I've died and gone to hell, thought Rose.

'Hey, are you awake? I've been waiting ages for you to wake up!'

Terrified, Rose disappeared under her covers. They were strange in themselves, no top sheet or blankets, just a light eiderdown.

With horror she realised that she herself was practically naked. All she had on was a long, thin vest and nothing else. Maybe I'm really sick, she thought, maybe this is some strange hospital or sanatorium – maybe I *did* catch diphtheria. She checked. She didn't feel sick, just scared. She thought about Mrs F and as she did so she realised for the first time that her right hand was clenched hard around the sharp points of the crystal. It's come with me, she thought. Wherever I've come to! In her mind's eye she saw Mrs F's button black eyes. 'Wish hard Rose!'

She screwed up her eyes and wished desperately to be back in her own bedroom.

'Are you okay? Is the music too loud? It's my alarm, I have to have it on max volume or I'd sleep through and be late for school. I'll switch it off.'

The room became suddenly silent.

It's no good, I'm going to have to come out, thought Rose. She stuffed the piece of crystal under her pillow, pulled down the eiderdown and peered across the room. A girl of about her own age was sitting up in a bed opposite her. She had short, red-brown hair that stuck out in a messy halo around her grinning face.

The strange girl spoke again, 'You're not at all like I expected you to be. I thought you'd be browner, and bigger.'

Rose's mother had always been very proud of Rose's pale complexion, she was never allowed to leave the house without a bonnet or, if it was sunny, a parasol. It was also true that she was rather small for her age. Her cousins were far taller, and Aubrey Perkins could rest his chin on the top of her head – something he was annoyingly fond of doing.

Rose felt she ought to reply to the strange girl, so she said, 'Oh,' because she really couldn't think of anything else to say.

The girl jumped out of bed. 'Come on, let's go and get breakfast. I'm starving and I think I can hear Mum downstairs in the kitchen. You must have arrived really late last night, 'cos I didn't hear you and I was trying really hard to stay awake. I even put marbles in my bed to stop me going to sleep.'

All the time she was talking, the girl was wandering round the room, taking off what looked like boy's pyjamas and putting on an odd selection of garments – no skirt or petticoats, no proper underwear that Rose could make out. Just a very short dress and some brightly coloured tights without any feet. Rose found it hard not to stare.

'Come on, Rose, I'm nearly ready. Are you really tired? Was it a long flight? What was it like? I've never been on a plane because Mum's really worried about the environment. It's *so* unfair, everyone else I know's been abroad except me, and who cares if the earth warms up? It'd be brilliant if it was like summer all year round. Was it really hot in Peru?' The girl finally took a breath and looked at Rose quizzically. 'You do speak English, don't you? Mum said you did.'

Rose nodded and, realising she couldn't stay in bed forever, she very gingerly swung her feet down and stood up, making sure her vest thing was pulled right down as she did so. The floor was almost completely covered in heaps of brightly coloured clothes and toys. They must be too poor to have a maid, thought Rose, but won't her mother be furious when she sees this mess?

The girl, however, seemed quite unconcerned and was busy pulling her hair back into a ponytail in front of a long mirror.

Rose wasn't allowed a mirror in her own bedroom in case it encouraged her to be vain. The only mirror she could reach was a small brass one hanging half way up the stairs. Because she was so small, she only ever got to see the top of her head. Nervously she sidled over to this one and stared at her reflection. The most shocking sight was her knees: thin, knobbly and pale as milk. The vest garment was purple with a vivid yellow design. She peered forwards. There were some words printed on it that she struggled to read in the reflection: *I'm A Little Cutie.* Rose was puzzled. What was a Cutie? Was this a hospital gown? Was Cutie a disease that she was suffering from?

She glanced across at the girl who had writing on her top as well. Hers read: *Perfect Princess.* Could it be *possible*? The girl didn't look at all like a princess and this small, cluttered room didn't seem like part of a palace.

'Come *on*, Rose, do get dressed. Your clothes are at the end of your bed. It must have been really hot in Peru for you to wear those shorts. Hey, are you okay? I'm sorry, I'm talking too much. Oh, and I'm really sorry about your Mum…' The curly haired girl tailed off and looked awkwardly at her feet. 'Shall I ask *my* mum to come up and see you? She's really nice when you're sad or upset.'

Rose realised she was going to have to make a quick decision. She could ask questions and admit that she hadn't a clue what was going on, or she could get dressed, go downstairs and try to work out what was happening for herself.

She took a deep breath. 'Please don't worry. I'll get dressed and come down now.'

Her 'clothes' were heaped in an untidy pile at the foot of her bed: first was a pair of tiny bloomers, then some extremely short stockings. Next she found what looked like a larger pair of bloomers, which she pulled over the top of the first pair. The only garment then left on the bed was a short sleeved vest in a very bright blue with the words *Smile* printed across it. It was very odd, thought Rose, the way all the clothes had writing on them. Was it a secret code? Did the words hold some sort of clue to what was going on? She looked around for the rest of her clothing but it was nowhere to be seen. Surely this couldn't be it? She was still half naked!

'Cool shorts. If you get cold you can borrow one of my jumpers. Your shoes'll be by the front door. Mum likes us to take them off in the house. It's a Buddhist thing. Let's go then.' The girl suddenly creased up her forehead. 'Did I say I was called Lily? I wasn't sure if you knew or not.'

Lily was already heading out of the room and onto a narrow landing. Rose, feeling horribly underdressed, followed her down a steep flight of stairs. There was no wallpaper on the walls but someone had painted a large rainbow that stretched right down to the hall below.

'Do you like it?' asked Lily, following Rose's gaze. 'Mum and I did it at a 'Get in touch with your inner rainbow' workshop.'

'Mmm,' replied Rose. She was still nervous of saying anything until she had a clearer idea what was happening.

The hall was a jumble of coats, shoes and a large collection of bags overflowing with balls of wool. It didn't look like a hospital and Rose was pretty sure by now that she wasn't sick – or dead. In fact it seemed to be just a small and very untidy house. The walls were covered in coloured photographs, mainly of Lily at different ages but nearly always wearing extraordinary-looking knitted hats. On a small table by the front door was a shiny, bronze statue that Rose recognised as a Buddha. When they'd lived in Clifton their elderly neighbour, Mrs Dainty, had one in her sitting room. It had a chuckling, fat face like a happy baby and Mrs Dainty had always told Rose to rub his tummy for good luck. Without thinking she went over and stroked the bronze Buddha's stomach. She needed all the luck she could get right now.

Lily had already marched down to the kitchen at the back of the narrow house, so Rose followed feeling increasingly nervous. She was not looking forward to meeting Lily's mother. She wasn't sure why, but she felt guilty, as though she'd done something wrong, although she didn't know what.

Rose had to screw up her eyes against the glare from the lights – electric lights! And in the kitchen! There were a few grand houses with electricity in Bristol, but not in small houses like this – and what was Lily's mother doing in the kitchen? Didn't they have a cook? Rose stared around the room. Every available patch of wall was covered in pictures – some of them just scraps of paper stuck straight onto the walls, some even looked like they'd been painted by Lily. A giant clock, like the one from Redland station, hung above a pine table covered in brown coffee stains and spots of milk. Piled up at one end of the table were stacks of magazines and papers. It was almost as untidy as Lily's room. It was far worse than Clara's, their last housemaid, who had been dismissed for being 'slatternly and slovenly' – and all she'd done was leave one petticoat on the floor.

'Rose, darling, how are you this morning? You were so tired

35

last night you could hardly speak!' A tall woman with a mass of red hair was standing by a stove stirring a large pan of porridge. She was wearing a stripy jumper and a long, tasselled skirt. As she looked at Rose she frowned for a moment, then smiled again. 'You do look *so* like Caroline. I didn't see it last night, but now I can – your eyes and hair are just like hers.'

Rose felt a wave of relief, as though she'd passed some sort of test – but what for? And how could she keep on passing?

'Sit down, darling. Is porridge alright for you? Everything must seem so strange and new for you.'

Well, *that's* certainly true, thought Rose, before replying, 'I'm fine thank you, m'am.'

Lily's mum looked at her oddly. 'Sylvia, darling, call me Sylvia.'

Rose had never in her whole life addressed an adult by their first name. But I must try to fit in she thought, at least until I know exactly where I am. 'Thank you very much – er – Sylvia. I always very much enjoy a bowl of porridge for breakfast.'

The rest of breakfast went reasonably well, Rose thought. She ate everything put in front of her, including some rather gritty bread and even drank up a vile-tasting orange drink.

'Carrot juice, darling, just packed full of vitamins.'

Rose had no idea what vitamins were but she guessed they were like cod liver oil – disgusting but good for you.

Just as they were finishing Sylvia glanced over at the clock. 'Ooh! We can catch the headlines if we switch on now.'

Lily groaned, 'But the news is *so* boring, Mum, can't we listen to something else? You're *always* listening to the news.'

Rose stared at Lily. Surely her mother would send her straight to bed for being so rude? But Sylvia completely ignored her daughter and reached over to press a button on a silver box on the mantelpiece.

To Rose's alarm a loud voice came straight out of it. 'And now for the nine o' clock news summary on Saturday the 2nd June, read for us today by Andrew Martin.'

So the date was the day after she'd wished in her bedroom. Rose was relieved – it meant she hadn't lost any time being ill and that she'd probably come straight here from her home. But how? And why couldn't she remember the journey?

The voice from the box carried on talking: about foreign wars, taxes, questions for the Prime Minister – all the usual news. But why had she never seen one of these talking machines before? Aubrey's father usually bought all the latest gadgets and Aubrey wouldn't have been able to stop himself from boasting about it. She was jolted back from her thoughts by a burst of music and then another announcement from the silver box: 'Brand new for Saturday mornings! Starting today – the 2008 Brain Box of the Year!'

Rose knew she must have misheard. Anxiously she looked around the room until she found what she was looking for – a calendar. 'Your Year for World Peace,' it read, and there was a picture of a lot of children in Indian dress waving cheerfully. In the middle of the page was today's date, just as it should be – Saturday 2nd June. But at the top, where it should have read 'In the year of our Lord 1898' it said quite clearly in large black print '2008'.

Exactly one hundred and ten years later.

Chapter Four

Brighton Street

'Why don't you take Rose round to the shops, Lily? It'll do you both good to get some fresh air and there are a few things I need from the store.'

Lily pulled a face. 'Okay, if I can get a comic whilst we're there.'

She took Rose out into the hall, where she quickly pulled on some shoes and flung open the front door. 'These are yours.' She thrust a pair of sandals at Rose. They were just a thin sole with two straps across and Rose struggled with the fastenings – she'd never seen footwear like these before. All the while her mind was boiling over with a million different questions – was it really 2008? Had she gone mad? Or was this a dream which she'd soon wake up from? Perhaps she really *was* sick and she was delirious? 'Please, where's my coat and gloves?'

Lily giggled. 'Come on, Rose. I know Peru's hot, but it's summer here you know. You won't be cold, I promise.'

With one leap, Lily jumped down the flight of steps and onto the pavement below. Rose followed placing her feet carefully on each step. She felt a warm breeze on her bare legs which was shocking and lovely at the same time. Then a small patch of sunlight fell onto her arm and it was like being bathed in a warm bath. 'I'm not going to worry about where I am and how I got here,' she thought. 'I'm just going to see what happens next – as though I was having an adventure in a storybook.' So, hatless, gloveless, coatless and *without* an adult, Rose and Lily set off up the road.

'What are all these carriages doing here?' Rose pointed at the rows of multicoloured vehicles that completely lined the street. 'Where do they keep all the horses?'

As soon as she'd asked, she wished she hadn't. Of course, these were the new-fangled motor cars. They didn't need horses. The Lord Mayor had one and so did the Fire Brigade, but not ordinary people. Maybe everyone was really rich now?

Lily looked at her quizzically. 'Did they have a lot of horses where you lived in Peru?'

Rose struggled with her conscience. She didn't want to lie – that would be a sin of course – but these were extraordinary times, so maybe God would let her off? And, if this *was* all a dream, surely lying didn't count in the same way as if you were awake?

'Yes,' she said.

For a few seconds Lily continued to stare at her, then she looked away crossly.

'You *can* talk to me you know. We're almost the same age, we could be best friends. I've been *so* looking forward to meeting you.'

Rose really did want to talk to Lily. She'd often longed for a sister or a best friend, but her mother never seemed to find other children 'suitable' and she didn't believe in sending girls to school. So there had been very little chance to meet anybody –she only saw

Aubrey and his brothers because they actually lived in her street.

'It's... um... just a bit difficult getting used to things. That's why I'm being a bit... er... quiet today – Aaargh!' Rose shrieked and grabbed at Lily's arm. One of the motor cars had just roared up the street, faster than a train, only a few feet from where they were standing.

Lily stared at her. 'Aren't you used to cars? Didn't they have them in your village in Peru?'

'It was a very small village.'

Rose hoped this wasn't a lie. But why on earth did Lily and her Mum think she came from Peru? And what had Lily had meant earlier, when she'd said she was sorry about Rose's mother? The only way it made sense was if they thought she was somebody else – someone also called Rose. But if that was true, what would they do when they found out she wasn't the girl from Peru? Would they be very cross? Would they send her to an orphanage? Or just throw her out onto the streets – by herself, in 2008 and in shorts!

I mustn't worry now, she reminded herself. I must just get on with it, do the best I can and keep on trying to work out what to do next. They had reached the top of the road and Lily turned right onto a larger street lined with restaurants and estate agents. There were a few shops dotted amongst them, but it was hard to see much of the road because of all the motor cars. As they walked along the pavement, they had to skirt around loads of upright black boxes surrounded by bags of rubbish. Rose stared around her. Everything looked familiar and yet different – the stonework and windows above the shop fronts were almost the same as in her time, but the shops themselves had garishly coloured signs and large flat windows. Then she gasped – across the road was the soaring bell tower, the arched windows, the craggy stone memorial to the drowned sailors of the SS *Malago*. It was St Saviours, it definitely was. A large blue banner hung outside the church porch:

LUXURY EXECUTIVE FLATS IN BRISTOL'S FINEST LOCATION – ONLY THREE REMAINING. VIEW NOW!

Rose was astounded. Surely people couldn't be *living* in the church? It *must* be a sin. The advertisement made her think of her father's posters. They'd been pasted all up and down the Whiteladies Road:

REDLAND VILLAS – THE DRAINAGE IS EXCELLENT AND THE NEIGHBOURHOOD HIGHLY RESPECTABLE. THE AIR IS SALUBRIOUS AND THE VIEWS EXTENSIVE AND PICTURESQUE.

'What does the salubi – thing mean, Papa?' she'd asked as they strolled up to the Downs.

'It means wonderful and clean – and no stink from the sewers and fish down by the docks!'

But the clear air hadn't been enough to persuade Bristolians to buy his houses and the rain had washed the posters into tatters, as one by one the new homes were boarded up.

Rose sighed as she gazed up and down the strange street. Then she saw something else she recognised – the butcher's!

Yeo Bros – Family Firm since 1890.

She ran across the road and peered through the window. A familiar-looking face glowered back at her.

'Oi! Don't smear the window pane, I just had it cleaned.'

The butcher shook a finger at Rose. He still wore a blue and white striped apron, but the straw boater with the red ribbon was nowhere to be seen. And now she could see him more clearly, it was obvious that he wasn't either of the two Yeo brothers, just someone who looked very like them. Lily was jigging up and down on the other side of the road, waving at her.

'Rose, don't run off like that – you'll get lost!'

Oh no I won't, thought Rose. I know exactly where I am – I'm in Chandos Road, in Redland, Bristol. In the year 2008.

The general store was an eye-opener for Rose. Lily took a basket and served herself from the shelves, and nobody told her off. The shop was lit by a very strong flickering light that hurt Rose's eyes. She could see apples, lettuces, tins of fruit – all stuff she recognised – but there were other mysterious looking items, with foreign names and strange curly writing on them. Everything seemed to be already wrapped up and something was missing, something important. It took Rose a little while to work it out. Of course! There was no smell. It didn't really feel like a shop at all.

'Do you like hummus and taramasalata?' Lily was waving some white pots at her. Rose panicked. Did she or did she not? She had no idea.

'I think so,' she tried.

Lily stared at her again with a puzzled expression. 'Well you must know – I won't get them if you don't like them.'

'Yes, thank you, do get them.' Rose thought it was probably more polite to say 'yes' than 'no'. Anyway she'd always been taught to eat everything put in front of her, whether she liked it or not. Lily placed both pots in her basket, still frowning slightly at Rose.

Next she picked up some milk in an odd, see-through container, before making her way over to a rack of small square books with shiny covers. The pictures on the front were coloured photographs. When Rose looked closer, she was shocked to see that some of the women were almost naked.

'Mum said we could choose a DVD. What would you like? You can choose, as it's your first day. I'll choose next time.'

Rose was determined to look like she knew what she was doing so she grabbed the first one she could find without a naked lady on it. 'I'll have this one.'

Lily looked surprised. 'Are you sure, I mean it's a bit young for you isn't it?'

'It's my favourite book. I love reading it.'

'Really? I didn't even know there was a book of it. I thought it was just on the telly.'

Rose groaned to herself. She'd done it again – given herself away – it was so hard not to make any mistakes. Lily was rather reluctantly putting the book that wasn't a book into the basket.

'Come on. Rose. Let's get to the till.'

They queued up with a scruffy group of people, most of whom, it seemed to Rose, were only half dressed. She was relieved to see that at least two of the women were wearing short trousers like her. As they waited, Rose looked over at the newspapers and magazines displayed on the shelf opposite. One headline in particular caught her eye, 'Prince's Fun in the Sun!' Underneath was a photograph of a young man in a tiny swimsuit, his arm around a lady who was hardly dressed at all. Rose's eyes widened in astonishment. What would the Queen say if she knew the Prince of Wales had been photographed like that? Then she remembered Queen Victoria would have died years and years ago. This must be one of her great, great grandsons! I've just got to get used to this, Rose told herself. For some reason, in the 21st century, people go around practically naked. Maybe it's got much warmer? Or maybe clothes have got more expensive? I don't know the reason, but I've just got to pretend it's all perfectly normal.

They walked back to Lily's house which, Rose could see now, was on Brighton Street. She recognised it as one of the little roads off Chandos Road, where she had visited the sick with Janetta. When they got in, Sylvia said she thought Rose looked rather washed out and pale.

'Why don't you sit down and watch a DVD. I don't normally let Lily watch telly in the mornings, but you did have a *very* long journey yesterday.'

Yes, thought Rose, much, *much* longer than you can imagine. Lily took her into the front room, which was just as cluttered as the kitchen. The walls were covered in pictures of people from India and there was a multicoloured rug hanging over the fireplace. Huge cushions were scattered over bare floorboards and Lily flopped down onto one of these in front of a square, black box. She took out the shiny book from the store and flipped it open. There were no pages inside, instead there was a silver disc which Lily snapped out and then posted into the bottom of the black box. She turned round and squinted up at Rose. 'Sure you want to watch this?'

Rose nodded and sat down carefully on a large, orange cushion. It was quite hard to know what to do with her legs. They looked very bare and white stuck out in front of her – she just wasn't used to seeing them, except perhaps very briefly in the bath. She decided to tuck them underneath her, which left her wobbling precariously on the top of her seat. Lily pressed a button on a slim silver object in her hand and a loud buzzing noise came out of the black box. Rose stared at the flickering lights that appeared on the front of the box. Maybe this would be like the slide show she'd seen at the Colston Hall? She had gone with her father to see Dr Clement Devereaux, Royal Astronomer to the Queen, and he had projected pictures of moons and stars onto a gigantic black screen. He had worn the most beautiful top hat that Rose had ever seen, and at the end of the lecture he had strode to the front of the stage and removed it with a flourish, the orange glow of the gas lamps bouncing off its shiny black brim. 'But this Ladies and Gentlemen, is only the start of our journey towards the stars and their meaning. Even with our wonderful modern telescopes, only a tiny fraction of our enormous universe can be seen. After that, a vast and endless space stretches away beyond the farthest reaches of our imaginations.'

His words had sent a delicious shiver of fear and pleasure through Rose, exactly like the one she was feeling now as she stared at the small screen. The box was suddenly filled with creatures of every colour imaginable, singing in strange high-pitched squeaks, laughing and dancing in odd, awkward jerks and spasms. Rose leant forward and put out her hands to touch them but her fingers crackled as they hit a glass screen. How did the creatures get in there? Were they fairies? Had Lily let them out of the silver disc and into the box? Rose was suddenly acutely aware of Lily staring at her from the other side of the room. Oh no! She'd done it again, behaved oddly, given herself away. The creatures continued to dance and sing. *We are the Chuckles, we're here to make you happee! We are the Chuckles, here's our bottle, here's our nappee!*

Rose was mesmerised. This was much, *much* better than any slide show she'd ever seen. It even beat Herr Blitz and his parachuting monkey at the Empire Exhibition. She wished she could ask Lily how it was done but she couldn't risk it.

Lily was sitting cross-legged on her bean bag, frowning at her. 'Do you really like this stuff? I mean it's just for little kids really. I used to like it when I was about three or four, but not now. Didn't you have many DVDs in your village?'

Rose didn't answer. Her mouth had fallen slightly open and she was staring fixedly at the box; she didn't want to miss one second of this wonderful show. Lily sighed, rolled off her cushion and wandered back into the kitchen where her mum was mixing up a bowl of oats for flapjacks. Lily loved her mum's flapjacks; they were always deliciously gooey and syrupy. She leant against her mum's arm, burying her head in the soft wool of her jumper.

'Mum, Rose seems… well… sort of a bit weird, you know – just sort of not how I expected her to be.'

Sylvia nodded. She knew just how much Lily had been looking forward to Rose's visit. Things hadn't been going very well for Lily, friend-wise, at school. It wasn't so bad at home because there were Freddy and Ellie next door to play with, but Sylvia knew what Lily really wanted was a best friend of her own age.

'Lily darling, it's a huge adjustment for Rose, coming to a new country. And she must be terribly worried about her mum. She doesn't know how long her mum'll take to recover or how long she's got to stay with us. She hasn't lived in this country since she was a little baby so everything must seem very different. They've no close relatives and Caroline's become such a recluse in the last few years. They really have been very cut off from normal life. So just try and understand if she seems a little odd – and be as kind to her as you can.' Sylvia gave Lily a big kiss and a hug.

Caroline Perkins had been Sylvia Staveley's best friend all the way through boarding school and, because her parents were divorced and lived abroad, Caroline had always spent the holidays with Sylvia's family. They'd stayed friends through college and even had their babies at the same time, both naming them after flowers: Lily and Rose. But Caroline had been restless and wanted to travel the world. Rose's father had left them soon after Rose was born so there was nothing to hold her back. So off Caroline had gone with baby Rose in her backpack and for the next three years Sylvia had postcards from India, China, Japan, Australia, New Guinea and finally, Peru. Caroline sent letters describing the tiny village where they were living, with the view of the high Andes Mountains in the distance; how she was setting up as a potter and just about making enough money for them both to live on. Then disaster struck – she got ill. She needed an urgent operation and time to recover afterwards, to get her strength back. She couldn't leave Rose all that time in the village and she could just about scrape the air fare together to send her back to the UK – would Sylvia take her? Of course she would.

Lily hugged her Mum back hard. 'Okay. I'll have another go at talking to her.'

When Lily had imagined what Rose would be like, she'd pictured a tough little girl, quite sunburned from living outside a lot. She had hoped she'd like reading books and making up games and stories – just like her. Instead Rose'd turned out to be a tiny pale thing who looked permanently terrified and hardly dared open her mouth. The only things she seemed really interested in so far were the butchers' shop and the Chuckles DVD. Lilv was afraid she was going to be hard work.

She walked back into the front room. Rose was now staring at a blank, slightly flickering screen. She turned to Lily, eyes wide:

'Can we watch it again?'

'No!' said Lily. 'Definitely not!'

The rest of the day was not much better. Lily helped Rose unpack, although Rose didn't seem to have a clue what was in her suitcase and kept saying 'Oh!' and looking amazed every time they took something out. They helped Sylvia make lunch and Lily thought Rose was really trying too hard to be helpful and polite. Then they went to the park which was a complete waste of time, as Rose didn't want to play on anything. She just stood by the railings staring across at the disused station buildings. Lily's next door neighbours, Freddy and Ellie, were there, but when they tried to get her to play football with them, she just looked confused and went and sat under the enormous oak tree that dominated the playground. She seemed more interested in the ancient milestone, now almost cracked in half by the tree's roots. It was actually quite a relief when it was time for bed and she could stop trying to entertain Rose or get more than one word out of her.

Rose was also glad to be safely tucked up in bed. She was exhausted. She'd had to get through a whole day watching every word she said, trying not to stare too much, trying to act as if she knew exactly what was going on. When really, she was feeling horribly lost and confused. All in all, She thought she'd done alright. She thought she'd got away with it so far – although the incident with the photo in the suitcase hadn't helped. It was in a silver frame, black and white, of a rather beautiful woman with long dark hair.

'Who's that?' Lily had asked, spotting it under a pile of clothes as they unzipped the case.

'I've no idea,' Rose had answered without thinking.

Just at that moment Sylvia had come into the room. 'Oh what a beautiful picture of Caroline. That must have been taken the year she left to go travelling – look she's still got her long hair!'

Lily had stared really hard at Rose then. Rose had frowned back at her, trying to will her not to say anything to Sylvia. It worked, but Rose was pretty sure Lily hadn't forgotten about it.

Now, as she lay in bed, her thoughts racing, her head aching with tiredness, she tried to force herself to keep awake: she must make a plan for tomorrow. What was the most important thing for her to do? What I really want to know is how I got here, she thought. And then how I can get back to my own time. If I can work that out I'll feel much better about being here. I've travelled one way in time, so surely there must be a way of going back? Then for a moment she thought about what 'back' meant: the sickness, the people she knew who'd died, the afternoon in the park, Aubrey, rollerskating – and what happened afterwards. But then if she stayed here and they found out about her, what would they do? She might be put in an institution and have her head shaved to stop the nits. Or worse, in a lunatic asylum with families coming for Sunday outings to gawp at her.

Rose yawned, her mind was getting muzzy and confused. It was no good she would have to give in and fall asleep.

'Rose, Rose!' She was torn back awake by Lily's urgent whisper. 'Rose, I know you're not really Rose at all. Are you?'

Chapter Five

Back To Cossins Place

Rose sat up in bed. She thought hard and quickly. 'I am Rose, but I'm not Rose Perkins. I'm Rose Cox.'

Rose couldn't see Lily's reaction in the dark. There was a long pause that seemed to last forever. Rose's heart hammered against her ribs. At last Lily spoke:

'Did you swap places with her on the plane? Or in Peru? How did you do it?' Lily's voice sounded surprisingly normal. A bit puzzled perhaps, but not really angry. I'm going to tell her, Rose decided. The room was almost black, there was just a slight orange glow from the streetlight outside, and somehow not being able to see Lily made her feel braver. I'm going to tell her. I don't think I can keep it a secret for much longer anyway, and it would make it so much easier for me if someone else knew. She clenched her fists and screwed up her eyes to give herself courage. 'I'm Rose Cox and I was born in 1887.'

'What! You're a little old lady then!'

'No! I'm a girl just like you, in fact exactly the same age as you. I'm eleven. I'm not older than you, I'm just from a different time.'

'So you're a ghost then?'

Rose felt quite taken aback. That possibility had never crossed her mind. 'I don't *think* so – I mean, I feel real and I don't think I've died.'

Or had she? Perhaps she *had* got ill and died that night, in her bedroom, as the tree scraped against her window? Rose quickly pushed that thought out of her mind. 'I believe I've travelled in time. I don't know *how*. But I used to live in Redland, very close to here.'

Lily was silent again. By squinting hard across the gloom of the room, Rose could just make out Lily's outline, sitting up in bed facing her. It seemed like ages before she spoke. 'I've been waiting my whole life for something like this to happen. I've read so many books about time travel and magic. I used to believe it could happen to me if I wished hard enough, but then I got older and stopped believing in all that stuff. You're not kidding me are you? It would be a really bad joke if you were.' Lily sounded breathless and a little cross.

Rose spoke up quickly to reassure her, 'No, no! It's all true, I promise. I'll even swear on the Holy Bible if you want me to. But *please* don't tell your mother or anybody else, I don't think they'd understand and I don't want to be sent away to a – a lunatic asylum.' Rose's voice trembled, she was on the edge of tears. It had been a very big risk telling Lily the truth. Could she really trust her?

'I don't think that would happen nowadays,' replied Lily. 'I think it's more likely you'd be put on the telly and have to give loads of interviews…' She stopped, guessing that idea wouldn't be very reassuring for Rose either. 'It's ok, I won't tell, but what are you going to do? How long are you going to stay? And where's

Rose Perkins gone?'

Rose looked alarmed. 'Oh my goodness! I've been so busy worrying about myself I never even thought of that.'

'Do you think you've really swapped places with her? That would mean she's gone back to your time!'

Rose felt a sinking feeling in her stomach. Suppose Rose Perkins caught diphtheria and died? It would be all her fault! Would that make her a murderer?

'Rose! Rose! Are you still there? I can't see you properly.'

A shaft of blinding white light hit Rose's eyes .She put her arm up to shield her face.

'Oops, sorry, didn't mean to scare you. It's just a torch – did you have them in your days? Wow! I've just thought – how did you cope with all that new stuff like the cars and the telly? It must have been so weird for you – and I thought you were just being a bit of a freak. Sorry!'

Rose didn't reply; she was still struggling with her conscience over sending Rose Perkins back in time. Lily carried on excitedly, 'I just love the Victorians! We're doing them at school at the moment. History's my favourite subject. I don't care if the other kids think I'm a geek. Hey! You'll be able to help me get really good marks in my project. Maybe that's why you came, 'cos I was reading so much about Victorian times, maybe I kind of conjured you up out of my imagination!'

Rose remained silent; Lily paused, then spoke in a low disappointed voice, 'It *is* all a joke isn't it? You *were* having me on – you're just like the kids at school – teasing me to have a laugh. Okay, you win. You got me.'

Rose heard her flop back down on her bed and pull the covers over her face. Rose thought for a moment and then crept over to Lily's side of the room. She squeezed her shoulder through the bedclothes. 'Oh Lily, it *is* true, I promise. I'll prove it to you.'

'How?' came Lily's muffled reply.

'There must be something I can show you, or tell you about, that I couldn't possibly have known if I wasn't a... um... Victorian. Let me think, Lily, and tomorrow I'll prove it to you. I do so want you to be my friend. I've never had a best friend before and I've always wanted one.'

Lily pushed a hand up from under the covers, found Rose's dark hair and patted it a few times 'Okay,' she yawned. 'See you in the morning.'

Rose woke early the next morning. She could hear a single bird singing outside and see a clear shaft of sunlight striking through the blinds onto the heaps of discarded clothes. The bedroom didn't seem quite so strange this morning. Lily had explained to her about the large eyed dolls on the blinds. 'They're off the telly – I've grown out of them really, but it's too expensive to buy a whole new blind. You mustn't tell the kids at school I've still got them though.'

Rose had promised. She was beginning to think the children at Lily's school sounded rather scary. As she lay in bed, she started to think about her promise to Lily the previous night. She had to think of a way to convince her she wasn't lying, but what on earth could she do?

She had worked out that Lily's house was on Brighton Street – a small road directly off Chandos Road. So that meant they were very close to Rose's old house on Cossins Place. Maybe there would be something there, something only Rose Cox could possibly have known about – something in the house or the garden. Rose racked her brain – surely the copper beech outside her window would still be there, her father had said they lived for hundreds of years. She remembered that quite clearly because her mother had groaned at the thought. 'Why didn't you get the builders to chop it down? It makes the dining room *so* dark and gloomy. I can't read without a lamp, even in the middle of the day. And it shades the garden so Cook can't have a decent vegetable patch.'

Mr Cox had sighed wearily. He felt tired all the time now. 'The builders were all local lads, they worked on the farms round here. They wouldn't touch the tree.'

The tree *was* enormous. It had grown when Redland was rolling farmland stretching up the hill to Westbury Village and Gloucestershire beyond. Once it had stood in a hedge of brambles and elder, shading cows and horses. Then the builders had come, hemming it in with tall houses and brick walls – but still it managed to stretch out its branches, to tap and scratch at Rose's window pane.

Rose tip-toed over to Lily's bed and shook her awake.

Lily snuffled and grumbled into her pillow. 'S'too early. Still asleep'. Then suddenly she sat bolt upright: 'Is it true what you were saying last night – or did I dream it?'

'It *is* true and I'm going to prove it to you. Get dressed and come with me. I'll show you something that'll make you believe it.'

'What, right now?' Lily squinted at her watch. 'It's five thirty in the morning!'

Milking time, thought Rose. 'Come on, Lily. We might see the cows coming down to the dairy if we're quick.'

Lily stared at her as if she was mad, then a broad grin spread over her face. 'The cows used to come down from Redland Green to be milked. I wrote about it for our local history project – you know, Rose, I'm starting to believe you already.'

'Don't they come down any more? Where do you get your milk from then?' Rose couldn't help feeling disappointed.

'Nope, milk just comes in bottles from supermarkets. You probably don't know what those are either do you?'

Rose shook her head. There was *so* much she didn't know, *so* much to get wrong. Without Lily's help she'd never get by in 2008.

A short time later they were walking up Brighton Street. Lily had left a note for Sylvia explaining their early morning walk. 'I've told her we wanted to watch the sunrise. She likes that sort of nature stuff.'

This time, Rose was able to look more closely at her surroundings. She wasn't so distracted by the cars, or the black boxes which Lily had explained to her were rubbish bins. Brighton Street was a narrow street stretching from Chandos Road down to the railway line. Rose had been there a few times with Janetta, who had a passion for visiting the elderly and sick. Janetta was probably about the most devout person Rose knew. Of course everyone *went* to church but Janetta would go up to four times a day on a Sunday, often travelling all over north Bristol to try out different services and vicars. Whenever she heard of a needy soul, she would rush round with chicken broths and colt's foot jellies, along with little cards printed with comforting religious thoughts. Mrs Cox had never been very keen for Rose to go with Janetta on these visits: she thought some of the homes were, 'Filthy! Infested with lice – or worse!' But her mother knew that Reverend Sylvester kept a watchful eye on his parishioners – particularly whether they were fulfilling their Christian duties to the poor. So every so often she would sigh and let Rose accompany Janetta on her rounds, 'For the good of your soul, but be sure not to shake hands or touch the furniture.'

It was obvious to Rose, when she went on these visits, that the houses were quite as clean as their own – it was just that they were smaller and had more people in them. On Cowper Road there were *eleven* little Dandos squeezed into Number 22.

'Where do they all sleep?' She'd asked Janetta as they delivered a parcel of Rose's old clothes.

'Well, you'll get at least four in a double bed – top to toe. You don't know how lucky you are having a bed all to yourself. I never slept alone until I came into service with your mother.'

It reminded Rose of the nursery rhyme, *There were ten in the bed and the little one said roll over, roll over...* Privately Rose thought it would be lovely to have someone to share her bedroom with, someone she could whisper and giggle with, rather than being all alone in her cold, green room. She'd skipped along, singing to herself: *So they all rolled over and one fell out and the little one said – Remember...*

'Miss Rose, you remember please: don't sing in the street! You know your mother wouldn't approve!'

Back in 2008 Rose was curious to see how Brighton Street looked now. As she looked around, something puzzled her: there was something missing – what was it? Then she realised. All the railings had disappeared. The shiny black-painted rails and gates that had proudly marked off the front gardens – they were all gone. Or almost gone, she could just make out the sawn-off stumps of rusted iron where they used to be. Some of the gardens still had walls, but the stones were flaking and bulging out at odd angles. The front gardens were taken up by black bins or, in some cases, by cars, parked right up against their sitting room windows. The doors on the houses looked different too: some of them were entirely made of glass and the windows around them were blank and curtainless. Rose looked up at one house and then gasped in horror: a man was standing at a mirror shaving himself, for the whole street to see, in nothing but his underwear!

'What's up, Rose. What are you gawping at?' Lily followed Rose's gaze upwards. 'Oh that's Dr Steele. He's a health nut, he always gets up early to cycle round the Downs. You'll meet his kids – they go to my school. Ellie's alright, she's only six, but Freddy's a pain in the butt. He's in my class.'

Rose had no idea what a 'butt' was. It sounded rather rude so she decided to change the subject. 'In my time we had railings. What's happened to them all?'

'It was the war. We had a huge world war, well two actually, and in the second one they took all the gates and railings to make them into aeroplanes or guns or something like that. My Gran says it was all a waste of time 'cos it turned out to be the wrong sort of metal and they couldn't use them any way. If you go onto Cossins Place you'll see people have spent tons of money putting them back again – Cossins Place is a posh road with lots of big houses in it.'

'*That's* where I wanted to take you. *That's* where I used to live! My house was Number 12. There's bound to be something there I can show you – something Rose Perkins couldn't possibly have known about – after all she's been in Peru for years, hasn't she?'

They turned onto Chandos Road, it was very quiet and still. Only one shutter was open – on the bakery – and a warm, bready smell wafted towards them.

'Mmm, doesn't it make you feel hungry?' Lily sniffed appreciatively. They walked on past an Indian restaurant and a Chinese takeaway, both smelling of spices and frying from the night before. A lone figure stood smoking in a doorway, still in his vest and slippers. 'Morning ladies, where are you to this early?' His pasty face and pale, ginger hair reminded Rose of someone but she couldn't remember who.

Lily sprinted off down the road. 'Just an early morning jog. We're entering the marathon you know.'

Rose had been told never to run in the street – too unladylike. Oh well, she thought, there's no one here to see me, and she set off after Lily. She was soon out of breath and panting. 'I can't keep up!' she gasped, bending over to get her breath back.

Lily walked back to her. 'You're not very fit are you? Didn't you do games at your school?'

'I didn't go to school.'

'You lucky thing!'

Rose shook her head. 'No, it was awful. My mother taught me and I never met any other children. I *so* wanted to go to school. They opened a girls' High School up at Redland Court and I used to watch them going up the hill to play games on the Downs.

I was *so* jealous; I begged my mother to send me there, but she kept finding excuses why she shouldn't. One time she said it was because the headmistress had been seen riding a bicycle!'

It was Lily's turn to shake her head in disbelief. 'I'd love it if my mum taught me at home – you don't know how lucky you were.'

Chandos Road led onto Fairview Drive, a short street dominated by a large pale-stoned chapel with beautiful arched windows. Rose pointed at it excitedly.

'It's the German Chapel, it's still here! I know this road, it used to be full of carriages on Sundays. German families came here from all over Bristol to go to church. They used to go for picnics up on the Downs afterwards. I always thought the children looked very jolly, but mother wouldn't let me talk to them because they were 'foreigners'.'

Lily stared over at the building. 'You know, I've never really noticed it before. I don't know anything about it, so I guess it doesn't really prove anything to me – is there something else you could show me?'

Rose led her on, past a long sweep of wall that took them round the corner and into Cossins Place. It was a wide road curving downhill to the railway line below. On either side tall, stone houses were set back behind smart driveways and well-kept front gardens. Rose stared up and down the road: it had a proper tarmac surface now and all the pavements were laid out, right to the bottom of the street where the stables used to be. These had been replaced with a row of low buildings with large, lime-green doors, some of which had words and symbols scrawled over them. Most of these she didn't recognise, but there was one bearing the mysterious message 'Banksy Rules OK.'

'Well, does it look any different?' Lily was hopping about from one foot to the other.

Rose wondered what to say. 'Um, well the street lights are different – they're sort of straighter and the tops are a lot smaller…'

'Oh come on, Rose. Don't talk about boring old lamps. What else?'

'Well, the roofs look different – what are all those spiky things sticking up out of the chimney pots?'

'TV aerials. What else?'

Rose gazed around. Actually so much was the same… maybe the stones and bricks were a bit darker and crumblier, a few of the front gardens had lost their walls, a lot of cars, less railings. Oh yes – there was something, something good, something she wished her father could have seen: 'All the houses are sold! There are people in all the houses!'

Lily looked at her as if she'd gone mad: 'Of *course* they are. Everyone wants to live here, it's one of the most popular streets in Bristol! Which was your house?'

Rose crossed the road and stood in front of Number 12. It still had a green door and the swan knocker was there with its outstretched wings and beautiful curved neck. The neck that fitted exactly into the palm of her hand when she rapped it; she could still hear Janetta's voice quite clearly in her head, 'Only two knocks mind, Miss Rose, or your mother will let us have it.'

I should have told Lily about the knocker before we got here, she thought, how silly of me! What else can I tell her about before we see it? I know, the copper beech tree! Excitedly she described it to Lily, telling her exactly how it had looked and where it was in the back garden. 'Of course it'll be much bigger now, but my father said they lived for hundreds of years – I'm sure it'll still be there.'

'We'll have to get closer,' said Lily, 'To try to see round the side and into the back garden.'

They tiptoed cautiously up the path. My gates have gone, thought Rose, and they've moved the plants around – the lavender used to be by the front door and the lilac tree has disappeared completely.

Lily was looking nervous. 'Rose, I'm not sure we should be doing this, people might think we're burglars.'

But Rose was filled with a new found confidence. What could go wrong? After all, she'd already travelled in time. Nothing could touch her now. They crept around the side of the house, but the way into the back garden was blocked by a high fence.

'Maybe if I stood on that rubbish bin I could get over.' Rose was already hauling herself up as Lily looked nervously on.

'*Please* be careful, Rose!'

Rose was teetering unsteadily on the edge of the bin, leaning forwards, trying to grasp the fencepost.

'Nearly got it – aargh!'

Rose overbalanced, her arms waving wildly, trying to grab anything she could to break her fall. She caught the top of the bin – and Lily's hair. Lily screamed and the bin crashed noisily to the ground shooting rubbish all over the path. Rose picked herself off the ground, rubbing her elbow and looking surprised. 'I nearly did it, my foot slipped at the last minute. Sorry, Lily, I'm not really used to climbing.'

But Lily was already half way up the drive. She turned back and gasped at Rose, 'Come on, they must have heard us. We've got to get out of here – fast!'

Rose followed reluctantly. She hadn't managed to show Lily the tree – or anything else that would prove who she was. As she ran after Lily she turned to look back at the house. She saw a hand appear around the bedroom curtains – pulling them back. For a moment, Rose's heart skipped a beat. Whose face would appear at the window? A stranger's? Or would it be her mother, standing at the window, staring down at her?

She whisked around, she didn't want to see – not yet.

Chapter Six

The Downs

When she caught up with Lily, Rose grabbed her hand. 'We can go back soon, can't we? If we can just get inside the house I can show you the garden and there are other things I can tell you about as well. Please, Lily.'

Lily looked anxious. 'I'm not breaking in – they'll already be suspicious after this morning.'

'Couldn't we just knock on the door and make up some reason to look round? Have they got children? We could say we were their friends. Do you know them at all?'

'Well, I know their kids are older than us, so that's no use. I know what the mum looks like – my mum sold her some of her hats a while ago. Maybe we could say we were researching a local history project. We'll have to wait though. It's far too early in the morning – and they might have seen us. If we go back, we'll have to wear different clothes.'

'Like a disguise!' Rose exclaimed.

'Maybe...' Lily said cautiously. Then she saw the bakery was open. 'Come on Rose, let's take some croissants back for breakfast.' She laughed at Rose's anxious expression. 'It's alright. They're really yummy!'

When they got back to Lily's house they found Sylvia in the hallway. She was frantically stuffing knitted hats into plastic bags and looking rather frazzled.

'Girls! Thank goodness you're back. We've got to be up on the Downs in ten minutes. Had you forgotten, Lily? It's the Natural Earth Festival and I've got to set the stall up before the traffic gets too heavy. How was the sunrise? Have you had your breakfast – if not, can you grab some fast? Sorry to rush you, Rose, I know it's only your second day here. But I booked for the festival ages ago and I'm hoping to sell lots of hats today.'

Sylvia stopped for a second and frowned at her reflection in the mirror. 'We really do need the money…' Then she turned round and saw Lily's anxious expression. 'No, no! Sorry darling, shouldn't have said that. We're doing alright, really.'

Rose couldn't make it out –were Lily and her mum rich or poor? They didn't have any servants, but Lily had told her they had a car and Lily had loads of clothes and toys. They had electricity, but her mum did all her own cooking and washing. And now she seemed to be saying she worked on a market stall!

Rose and Lily munched the croissants as they followed Sylvia out of the house. Lily was right – they really were delicious.

'I'm afraid we'll have to take the car,' Sylvia sighed. 'I don't like to for such a short journey, but we'll never get all this stuff up there otherwise.' She stopped in front of a rather battered-looking vehicle. Rose couldn't help feeling a little disappointed – there were much smarter ones parked around it. Still, she had never been in a motor car before, and only once on a train, when she was very small and could barely remember it. Sylvia loaded up the car with bags and boxes, all overflowing with extraordinary-looking woolly hats.

'Do you like knitting, Rose?' she asked as she shoved another load into the boot.

'I do, very much.' Rose was relieved to be asked a question that she could answer truthfully. 'I'm knitting a scarf. I'm rather slow I'm afraid. Janetta always says there'll be snow in Africa before I finish.'

Sylvia looked interested. 'Is Janetta a friend from your village?'

'Um, sort of...' Rose blushed, she really hated all this lying. Thank goodness she didn't have to lie to Lily any more.

'Did you bring the scarf with you?'

'No.' Rose was able to reply truthfully.

'Well, darling, if you want to start again we've got the most marvellous wool shop just around the corner on Chandos road. It's a little old – fashioned but they sell everything you could ever need there.'

Rose felt a prickly feeling run up and down her spine. 'The wool shop'... 'Everything you could ever need'... Could it be true? Was it really still there? Well the butcher's and the baker's were. Maybe it wasn't so surprising that the wool shop was too. Why hadn't she seen it when she was out with Lily? She must have been so distracted by all the new things that she'd missed it. Rose knew she should go and find the shop, if not now, then soon.

Lily was tugging at her sleeve urgently. She pulled her a little way up the street then whispered in Rose's ear. 'Have you ever been in a car? Will this be your first time?'

Rose nodded. 'But I did see the Lord Mayor go by in one at the Queen's Diamond Jubilee celebrations. It looked a bit different to these ones, though. His was much bigger and it didn't have a roof.'

'I'll try and help you with the seat belt and stuff like that. Just try not to look too puzzled and for goodness sake, don't scream or anything like that.'

They all piled into the car; Rose managed her seat belt with Lily's help. Sylvia settled into the driving seat, a woolly hat jammed well down over her head.

'Off we go!' she called back to the girls and then stamped her foot down hard on the accelerator. The car shot forwards – and Rose screamed.

They crawled up through the traffic on Whiteladies Road and eventually found a parking space on the Downs where they could unload the stuff for the stall. Rose had managed to convince Sylvia that she'd screamed because Lily had stood on her toe. She'd been very relieved that the rest of the journey had been at a snail's pace. Even so, the whole car thing had made her feel quite sick and she was glad to get out into the fresh air on the Downs. They looked much barer than she remembered. Many of the trees and bushes had disappeared, and the grass was criss-crossed with tarmac paths. She looked around for the sheep nibbling at the rough grass, but they were nowhere to be seen.

Rose's mother had never been keen for her to go up to the Downs. 'It's a hideout for pickpockets and thieves – and goodness knows what other riff raff!' But Rose and her father had loved to ride round them in the horse and carriage, just the two of them, laughing and singing as they racketed over the pot holes. She'd really hated it when they'd had to sell the horses. It had been the worst thing about her father losing his money.

Sylvia and the girls carried the boxes over to a group of white tents. A huge banner hung over them: *Welcome To The Natural Earth Festival. Inner Peace For Your Body and Mind.*

Sylvia stopped in front of a trestle table with a rainbow coloured awning. 'This is our stall. Will you help me lay out the hats girls? Then you can have a wander around.'

Rose lined up the most colourful ones at the front. She was puzzled by the price tags. Ten pounds? Surely nobody in their right minds would pay that much for a woollen hat?

'Do you think your mother is going to sell any thing?' she asked Lily worriedly.

'I hope so, she hasn't been doing very well lately – the weather's been too warm. And I think she's worried about paying bills and the stupid mortgage thing...' Lily trailed off. She didn't really like talking about personal stuff. But Rose smiled and slipped her hand into Lily's.

'I know. It's awful when your parents worry about money and houses. It gives you a kind of sick feeling in your stomach, doesn't it?'

'Yes, that's exactly it, but how do you know? You lived in a big house with tons of servants and things.'

'Well, we *were* rich. We had a really enormous house over in Clifton. But actually I hated it. My nursery was right at the top and nobody ever came up there, and I was hardly ever allowed downstairs. I was quite glad when Papa lost his money and we moved to Cossins Place. It meant I didn't have to have a nursery and I was much closer to the kitchen, so I could listen to Janetta and Cook talking.'

'How did he lose all his money then?'

'Building Cossins Place. He used all our money and then

when he couldn't sell all the houses, he had to borrow money from Mama's family. It was terribly shaming for him. I wasn't supposed to know, but I'm very good at listening behind doors.'

Lily considered this for a moment. 'My mum had to ask my dad for money, they were always rowing about it. But now he's gone to live in America and we don't hear from him at all.' She saw Rose's puzzled expression. 'Oh, they're divorced. Did you think he was dead or something?'

'Well, yes,' Rose looked down at her feet. 'I suppose that must be terribly shaming for you – them being divorced I mean. It's alright, I promise I won't tell anyone.'

Lily giggled. 'Don't be silly. Nobody cares about that stuff now.'

Sylvia waved an enormous orange hat covered in pink bobbles. 'I can never seem to sell this one. Would you like it, Rose?'

'No, thank you very much,' Rose answered honestly.

'Well, thanks for all your help, girls. Why don't you go for a wander round and I'll see you in about half an hour.'

Lily started to race off. 'Come on, Rose. Lets find a food stall. I'm starving.'

Rose followed her, treading carefully over the tussocky grass. Lily was dodging in and out of a host of little stalls. Rose peered at the signs hanging above them: *Crystal Healing – your Pathway to the Real You... Self-knowledge through Weaving... Single Mothers against Whaling.*

Rose tried hard to work out what they could mean, but it was no use, she would have to ask Lily. When she caught up with her she was standing in front of a food stall. A banner above it read *Earth Food From The Soil.*

'Ugh! Who would eat that?' Rose thought. It sounded quite disgusting. But Lily thrust a sticky brown slice into Rose's hand.

'It's a chocolate brownie – don't pull a face, it's really delicious.'

Rose tried a mouthful. It really was gorgeous, it didn't taste like soil at all. The man serving at the stall was brown skinned with masses of plaits and beads in his hair. Rose tried not to stare.

'Has he come all the way from Africa?'

'*No*, he's British. His family probably came here years ago. I think people travel about a lot more now than they did in your time.

People were starting to flood into the festival and Rose could see she was right. There were women covered up from top to toe in black robes and others who were nearly naked. Some had masses of jewellery and others looked more like tramps. Some looked like gypsies with tattoos and pierced ears – even noses! There were families with prams and balloons and there were children dressed up as fairies and pirates. A brass band started to play in the centre of the tents and everyone crowded round to watch and clap. Then a fire-eater came out and blew hissing clouds of flame. Rose felt almost drunk with excitement; she had never been allowed to go to the fairs on the Downs. Aubrey had, and he'd boasted to her about the jugglers and magicians that he'd seen up there – and now here *she* was, right in the middle of it all.

Rose felt a pang of guilt. Here she was enjoying herself and Aubrey had been left behind in her own time, maybe dying. Rose wished Aubrey was here so she could see if he was safe. And she couldn't help thinking that he'd be a little bit envious of her actually helping out on one of the stalls. Oh, the stall! They'd promised to be back in half an hour. Rose looked around for Lily – she was nowhere to be seen.

Rose pushed through the crowd; it was so thick now and she was so small, all she could see were arms and legs. Which way had they come? Rose looked around anxiously. If she could only find the Crystal Healing sign, she could work her way back to Sylvia's stall. People kept bumping into her and the steady thump of the music throbbed through her head. She started to feel sick from the chocolate brownie and dizzy from the heat and noise. Oh please let me find my way back, please! Rose squeezed her eyes tightly shut as she wished.

'Are you alright, my lovely?' Someone was gently tugging at her arm, pulling her back into a quieter space behind the stalls. It was a woman's voice and sounded kind and vaguely familiar. Rose opened her eyes. The noise and bustle had receded to a faint background hum. They were standing on a patch of grass; in front of them was a low, odd-shaped tent. Before she knew it Rose was being guided firmly inside it.

'Come in and have a sit down, lovely. I'll brew us some nice green tea while you recover yourself. You just got a bit hot and bothered didn't you? You'll be right as rain in a bit and then I'll get you back to the hat stall.'

'Thank you very much for rescuing me, and the tea – but how did you know which stall I was from? I don't remember seeing you before.'

'Don't you, dearie? Oh, I was there – you were just too busy to notice me maybe.'

It was dark in the tent, but as her eyes got used to the light, Rose could make out the outline of the woman sitting opposite her.

She was dressed in layers and layers of orange clothing; her skirts were decorated with hundreds of tiny mirrors and fringed with long tassels that brushed against her ankles. She had grey, shoulder length hair and, despite the fact she was old, it was full of clips and ribbons. She was bending forwards over a little gas stove and as she lit the flame, Rose could see that the walls of the tent were covered in pictures of elephants, monkey gods and many-armed, half-naked women. Rose was alarmed. Janetta would definitely call this a heathen place and Janetta had warned her about heathens: 'They worship devils and eat little Christian children like you for breakfast.' Rose shivered and watched the old woman carefully as she brewed the tea. She's quite small, thought Rose, I could easily overpower her if she tried to grab me. But suppose she's planning to drug me with the 'green tea'?

'If you don't mind I won't have any tea after all, thank you.'

The old lady looked surprised. 'Well, alright lovely, you just looked like you could do with a bit of perking up. I'll have a cup myself and you have a little rest. I'm quite done in – I've been reading all morning.' She sat back with a sigh on a mound of cushions. Reading didn't strike Rose as a very tiring occupation. She loved to read and never seemed to get enough opportunity to do it – her mother was convinced it would 'strain her eyes'. The old woman was staring at Rose thoughtfully.

'Would you like me to do a reading for you? It'll be free mind – I won't charge you this time. I think you'll find it interesting.'

So she'd meant reading *fortunes* not books. Rose wasn't sure what to say; Cook had had her fortune told once and had been told she'd marry a sailor. 'That was forty years ago and I'm still waiting!'

Then of course there'd been that time in the wool shop…

'Alright,' she said primly. 'But I am expected back very soon.'

'That's fine, lovely, don't you worry. Now if you come a little closer so I can see your face…'

She patted the floor in front of her and Rose sat down. A flash of anxiety went through her mind – was the old woman planning to hypnotise her? Aubrey had seen a man who'd been made to bark like a dog when he was hypnotised. She didn't want anything like that happening to her.

'Now, dearie, take a few deep breaths – in and out, long easy breaths. That's right, let your mind empty itself of all thoughts and worries. Very good, keep breathing – in and out, in and out…'

Rose felt dreamy and relaxed. It was difficult to totally empty her mind. Odd things kept popping into it: the swan door knocker, the Chuckles, Janetta's Sunday hat, Aubrey bent over struggling for breath – oh no! She didn't want to think about that. She didn't want to think about anything to do with that day. She snapped open her eyes, suddenly wide awake and desperate to get out of the tent. Every wall seemed to be covered in hangings. Where was the entrance. How had she got in? Rose got to her feet and tried to feel her way around the sides, pushing at the heavy material, trying to find an opening.

'Now lovely, it's alright, don't run off.'

The old lady was struggling to her feet, following her. She caught hold of Rose just as she found the curtain hiding the door. As she lifted the flap, sunlight streamed in and Rose could see the woman's face clearly for the first time. She was looking at Rose hard with piercing, endlessly black eyes. 'You can't run forever Rose. There has to be some time or place where you stop and face your fears.'

Rose stared back at her. She had that prickly feeling again, up and down her spine. The old lady gave her a quick shove out onto the grass.

'Quick now. You don't want to be late. Go out between those two stalls and turn left – you can't miss it.' The old woman turned to go back inside her tent, then called after her once more. 'And don't forget your promise, Rose Cox.'

The noise from the fairground surged towards her as she ran back into the crowd, and in no time at all she found herself standing in front of Sylvia's stall.

'Where have you *been* darling? We've been so worried about you. Lily says you just disappeared. You must try and stick together. There's such a crowd here and some of them are quite odd types.'

Oh yes, they certainly are, thought Rose. But something held her back from telling them exactly what had happened. She still felt shaken up by her experience. There had been something familiar about the old lady and yet unfamiliar – she couldn't quite put her finger on it. She had seemed to know something about Rose – about how frightened she was of dying of diphtheria. There was something else though, something bigger and more important, something so strange Rose could hardly bear to think about it. The old lady had called her by her real name. She'd called her Rose Cox.

CHAPTER SEVEN

Saint Philip and Saint James

Rose and Lily were walking up Chandos Road, away from the church and out towards Whiteladies Road and the Downs. They were each carrying a rucksack on their back and a drawstring gym bag. Rose was almost sick with fear and excitement; Lily just felt glum. What on earth were the other kids going to make of Rose? They teased her enough as it was, making fun of her mother and her weird hats. They made gagging noises when she brought in her mum's gooey flapjacks and refused to buy the odd-shaped cakes that Sylvia sent in for the weekly cake stalls. The worst time of all, of course, was the day her mum had volunteered to do a knitting workshop for Lily's class. It had taken Lily weeks to get over that one.

Lily had a habit of trying to find the quietest, most tucked away bit of the playground. There she would curl herself up into the smallest place possible and try to read her books in peace. It never worked though, some boy would always manage to kick a football right into her face or climb up on the wall and drop grass cuttings on her hair. Lily *had* had a friend once, called Marnie. They could chat for hours at a time, making up stories and games together. Lily had never had to worry about playtime with Marnie around. But then Marnie's dad had got a new job in Scotland. Scotland! It couldn't have been any farther away from Bristol. There was no chance of ever seeing her again. That had been two terms ago and Lily had hated school ever since. All the other girls thought making up stories was babyish, they liked talking about hair or who was going out with who.

They were nearly at school now. Lily glanced nervously over at Rose. How was she going to manage? She'd never even been to school in her own time! Lily was going to have to keep a very strict eye on her; she'd need to cover for any obvious mistakes that Rose might make. It was strange, so far the adults that had met Rose hadn't seemed to notice anything particularly odd, apart from saying what 'lovely manners' she had. But Lily knew that kids would be a lot harder to fool.

They arrived at the school gate, where a large sign showed smiling children holding hands around a sunflower with the words: *Welcome to St Philip and St James School – Learning Happiness Together.*

Underneath someone had scrawled 'Phil and Jim Loony Bin' – which seemed to Rose to be a bit rude.

Rose suddenly started to feel very nervous indeed. She followed Lily into the playground and was instantly hit by a wall of sound. It sounded like hundreds of children all screaming at once and, looking around, Rose realised that was exactly what it was. Everyone seemed to be running and yelling at the same time. Boys were waving their bags around their heads like lassoes, footballs spun through the air, small girls on tiny scooters swooped into one another. None of them were taking the slightest bit of notice of the adults, who huddled together in small groups round their pushchairs and dogs.

'Well this is it, this is my school. It should be St Philip and St James, but we all call it Phil and Jim.' Lily waved her arm towards a low red-brick building. Rose thought it looked quite welcoming and friendly. 'Rose, *please* try and remember everything I've told you. Don't say anything unless you really have to. You're from Peru, but you don't want to talk about it, 'cos you're upset about your mum. *And* you don't want to talk about her either, 'cos you're…well, upset. Okay?'

Lily stopped talking. A group of girls from her year had spotted them and were coming over. They crowded round and started firing off questions. Who was the new girl? Where was she from? How long was she staying for? Rose did her best to follow Lily's instructions. She nodded her head a lot and left most of the talking to Lily. She listened hard to the way the other girls talked so she'd be able to copy them later. She'd already worked out that 'okay' meant yes, but they kept saying things were 'cool' and 'wicked' in a way Rose found very puzzling. Why did coming from Peru make her wicked? Why did they think it was cool there when Lily had told her it was very hot?

A shrill whistle brought the whole playground to a sudden halt. For a moment everyone froze, then there was a mass charge up to the school doors. Rose ran with the rest of them. She'd waited all her life to go to school and she didn't want to miss a minute of it. Amazed at Rose's enthusiasm, Lily jogged after her.

'Line up quietly, children, and go in – *without* shoving, Tom! And that means you too, Alfie. No running in the corridors, Alisha…'

A young woman in trousers and T-shirt ushered Lily's class into a large, brightly-decorated classroom. Surely that can't be the teacher, Rose thought. She knew clothes were different now but she'd been expecting at least a skirt, possibly even a hat. And where was her cane? Aubrey was always telling gruesome stories of being 'whacked by the beak'. Rose wondered if they still called teachers 'beaks'. The boys had called them that because they looked like old crows in their black gowns, but there was no sign of gowns or canes at Phil and Jim.

'Rose, I'm Miss Wright. Come up to the front and I'll introduce you to the class.'

Rose went up to stand by the teacher and smiled politely at the other children. Lily sat down at her table feeling extremely nervous. Please, please don't let her say anything weird, she wished.

'Rose here has come all the way from Peru. Which is very exciting for us as she'll be able to tell the class all about it in Show and Tell this afternoon – won't you Rose?'

Rose nodded her head vigorously, whilst Lily groaned inwardly to herself. Miss Wright led her over to Lily's table. Rose was rather disappointed that she didn't get a desk of her own, but she did get a shiny new pen, although the nib seemed rather small for dipping in an ink well. She turned the pen around in a quizzical way.

'Are you alright, Rose? Would you prefer a pencil?'

'Oh no, this will do very well thank you,' replied Rose politely.

A couple of the boys snorted into their hands and Miss Wright reminded them that Rose was new and they must all be very kind to her. Rose decided that she liked Miss Wright very much indeed.

She didn't seem at all strict and every time Rose looked at her she smiled back in a friendly way. Rose thought Aubrey must have been exaggerating when he'd told her his school masters threw board rubbers at them and slammed desk lids on naughty boys' hands.

Rose watched the other pupils and found her new pen worked without needing to be dipped in an ink well. In fact, it flowed beautifully without making the wretched ink blots that spattered her work at home.

To her surprise, Rose found the reading and writing tasks quite easy. Miss Wright was particularly pleased with her handwriting and held it up for the whole class to see.

'This is classic English copperplate writing, girls and boys. I didn't know they still taught it anywhere. That's wonderful, Rose. Keep it up!'

Rose did equally well with her tables, and was quite shocked that Lily still stumbled over hers. There were, however, a few lessons that were completely new to her – and rather puzzling.

'Circle Time!' Miss Wright called out, half way through the morning. They all sat cross legged on the floor in front of her. Some of the children were whispering and giggling and had to be reminded that this was a very important part of the day and that they must behave. Then Miss Wright looked very solemn, as if she was about to pray.

'Now today we are going to talk about what makes us sad. Saffron you can start. Alfie, if I have to tell you again to be quiet, you'll get a red card!'

Rose wondered if this was code for a caning but a few minutes later, when Alfie started whispering again, all the teacher did was hand him a red-coloured card. Rose was quite disappointed, but it did have the mysterious effect of shutting Alfie up. Meanwhile, a short, stubby girl had stood up and was telling the class that she felt very sad when her little sister 'drawed on my arm'. The other children, particularly the girls, all nodded their heads sympathetically.

'Now Rose, would you like to have a turn? What makes you unhappy?'

Rose answered quickly, without having to give it any thought, 'My father dying.'

Lily put her head in her hands.

Miss Wright looked concerned. 'I'm so sorry Rose. I didn't know you'd lost your father.'

Rose realised she'd made a serious mistake.

'Well he's not really dead. He's, um, er, sort of… well… gone…' She tailed off realising she was just making things worse.

'Don't worry, Rose. It's been a difficult time for you, I know. Thank you for sharing with us.' Miss Wright was looking at her so kindly that Rose felt tears starting to well up in her eyes. I mustn't cry here, she thought and clenched her teeth to stop the tears.

'Well, I think we'll stop Circle Time now and move into the gym for some dance,' announced Miss Wright brightly.

Relieved, Rose followed the others into the school hall, which doubled as the gym. Lily caught up with her and gave her a meaningful frown.

Rose frowned back. 'I am doing my best, you know Lily. Anyway, if they think I'm odd, they'll think it's because I'm from South America.'

'Well, yes, exactly. And now you've gone and agreed to talk about your life in Peru for Show and Tell!'

'I was just being polite. What *is* Show and Tell?'

Lily groaned. 'We'll just have to work on your story at break-time. Maybe there'll be something about Peru in the library.'

'Thank you, Lily. I really don't know what I'd do without you.' Rose gave Lily's hand a squeeze.

'That's okay. Look, you can stop holding my hand now. The other kids are staring at us. When we're doing dance, try and follow what I do, alright?'

'Okay.'

Rose enjoyed the dance class. It wasn't anything like the waltzes and polkas that she'd learnt with her cousins. Miss Wright put on a very loud song and the children ran around wherever they wanted to, waving their arms and rolling their heads about. Rose joined in enthusiastically.

'How did I do?' she whispered breathlessly to Lily at the end.

Lily looked like she wasn't really sure. 'Well, you weren't as bad as some of the boys, but you didn't need to jump up and down quite so much – and it was meant to be in time with the music.'

Lily had given Rose quite a lot of coaching about lunchtime and on the whole it passed off reasonably well. Although it was obvious to the dinner ladies that Rose had far better table manners than any normal child. Rose thought the food tasted rather odd. It was very salty and even the main course tasted sweet. But she really enjoyed the chips, which she'd never been allowed at home.

The long playtime after lunch was more of a challenge. Lily's plan had been to keep Rose as far away as possible from the other children, to reduce the risk of her giving herself away. Rose's plan, however, was to make as many friends as possible. She had waited a long time to go to school and she wasn't going to be stuck by herself in some corner of the playground. Before Lily could stop her, Rose rushed up to a cheerful – looking girl with short brown hair and sparkly glasses.

'Hi, I'm Rose. I'm okay. Are you cool?'

Rose felt very pleased with herself. She'd used not one but three modern words. She ignored Lily, who was frantically signalling at her to stop. Rose could see the girl looked surprised, but she answered Rose in a friendly voice.

'I'm Amy. It's pretty cool coming from Peru. Do you get to ride llamas?'

'Yes, thank you for asking. Nearly everyday.' It was frightening, thought Rose, how easily she could lie now and hardly feel guilty at all. Lily was now waving dementedly, but Rose was determined to carry on.

Lily slunk away to her usual hideaway, peering out every now and then to see an ever-growing crowd around Rose.

'Lily, come over here, we're just about to start a game!' Rose was jumping up and down excitedly. 'It's called Queenie, Queenie. I've been teaching it to them, we just need to find a ball and we can start.'

Amy and Saffron ran off to ask the teacher for a ball while Rose went through the rules again. 'We pick someone to be Queenie, and she stands with her back to everyone else and throws the ball over her shoulder. Then one of us catches it and hides it behind our back. Queenie turns round and we all sing at her – *Queenie,*

Queenie who's got the ball? Are they short or are they tall? Are they hairy or are they bald? You don't know 'cos you don't have the ball! Then Queenie has to guess who has the ball and the last person to be picked is the new Queenie.'

They played it for the rest of break-time. Lily was surprised how much she enjoyed herself and no-one teased Rose, or her, the whole time. Before they knew it, the bell went for afternoon lessons.

As they lined up, Lily gave out a groan. 'Rose, we completely forgot to look up about Peru in the library!'

'Don't worry, Lily.' Rose was full of confidence after her success in the playground. 'I'll be able to make something up.'

'Well Rose,' said Miss Wright. 'We've all been dying to hear from you about life in Peru. Would you like to start off the 'Show and Tell' for us?'

Rose stood up and gave a beaming smile to the class. She really was enjoying school life. It wasn't nearly as scary as Aubrey and Lily had made out. She took a deep breath and spoke very loudly and clearly. 'I come from Peru which, as I'm sure you know, is a land full of heathens. They worship heathen gods and eat little children. Not all the time though. They didn't eat me of course, otherwise I wouldn't be here talking to you.'

Some of the children began to snigger and Miss Wright looked a little anxious.

Rose continued bravely on. 'My mother and I tried to bring Our Lord's teachings to the poor people of the village. Many's the day we would sit in our mud hut reading passages from the Bible to them. Unfortunately for us, the local people did not wish to hear our message and one of them shot poor mama with a poisoned arrow. Even now, she is languishing on her sickbed, whilst I, thank God, have been brought back to the safety of our mother country. God Save The Queen!'

Rose sat down. She felt very pleased with her performance. She'd kept it short and to the point and she didn't think she'd said anything out of the ordinary. She'd mentioned God, which she knew adults *always* liked you to do. *And* she'd managed to put in a patriotic salute at the end. All in all, a very successful speech, she thought.

There was quite a long silence after she sat down, broken only by a few nervous giggles from the other children. Rose looked over at Lily, but her face was buried in her hands. Miss Wright also had a rather strange expression on her face. Rose began to feel less confident. Perhaps she had gone a *teeny* bit over the top with that part about the poison arrow.

Miss Wright coughed a few times and looked around the room. 'Well, er, thank you, Rose. That was a very, um, interesting talk. You obviously have a strong faith, which I hope will be helpful to you in this difficult time.' She paused, still looking rather flustered. 'Now, class, who else would like to do a 'Show and Tell'? Ah, Robert, you've been to the dentist today. Why don't you tell us all about it?'

Rose thought Robert's account of the dentist's chair going up and down and his having to spit out funny pink liquid, was rather dull compared with her talk, but Miss Wright seemed very pleased with it.

'Now class that was very reassuring, wasn't it? We don't need to feel scared about going to the dentist anymore, do we?'

* * *

On the way out of class, at the end of school, Amy and Saffron came over to Rose. 'Your 'Show and Tell' was brilliant! They're usually *so* boring. You will do some more, won't you?'

They linked arms with Rose and she felt a warm rush of happiness. She hadn't felt this good since her rides round the Downs with her father. He'd race the horses along, jolting over the rough ground, Rose's bonnet nearly flying off, her face snuggled against his fur collar, and both of them laughing. His laugh was deep and growly, hers a helpless giggle of fear and delight.

Chapter Eight

Number Twelve

'How was your first day, Rose darling?' Sylvia was kneading dough energetically on the kitchen table. The flour had spread like long white gloves up her arms and was dusted over her face and hair. Even so, the girls could tell she'd been crying.

'I had a really nice time, thank you very much.' Rose could tell Sylvia wasn't really listening so she didn't go into all the details of the day. She looked over at Lily to see if she might know what the matter was, but Lily was looking anxiously at her mum.

'Are you okay mum?' Lily went over and laid her head gently against her mother's shoulder.

'I don't want you to worry, Lily, it's just grown up stuff. Oh, and it's alright Rose, its nothing to do with your mum. In fact, I've got some good news about that. I had a phone call from the hospital to say her operation went well and she's recovering really quickly. You may be able to go home by the end of the month.'

Rose felt guilty. She hadn't been worrying about Rose Perkins' mum at all. In fact, she'd been enjoying herself so much, she hadn't even thought about Rose Perkins and the danger that she might be in. As for going 'home' at the end of the month, that raised so many scary questions that Rose pushed it firmly to the back of her mind.

Lily was still cuddled up against Sylvia. '*Please* tell me what's wrong mum. You're not ill are you? Or is it the money? I know I'm rubbish at knitting, but I could do some posters for you. And p'rhaps Rose could manage some easy hats – what do you think, Rose?'

Rose nodded, eager to help out. Although actually her knitting skills were limited to stringy – looking scarves and holey socks. Sylvia sighed. She stopped kneading the bread and stared, for what seemed like hours, at the wall in front of her.

'Sit down girls. I've got something to explain to you. It's quite hard for me to tell you this, but I think you're probably old enough now.' She sounded very serious and sad, not at all like the normal Sylvia. And she hadn't called them 'darlings', which couldn't be a good sign. Both Rose and Lily got nasty sick feelings in their stomachs. She's found out I'm not really Rose Perkins, was Rose's first thought. Maybe she's called the police! Lily was thinking, it's the house, she's got behind with the rent and we'll have to move and I don't want to leave, I love this house.

They all sat round the cluttered pine table. Sylvia took a deep breath, looked up at the ceiling and then down again at her clasped hands. 'Girls, when I was much younger I did something I'm very ashamed of – something I've always told you not to do. Myself and some friends started taking drugs. You know, the ones you've been warned about at school. One day, the police came to our house and searched it. I was the only one in at the time and they arrested me and took me down to the police station…'

'Did you go to prison?' Lily burst in.

'Just for a very short time. And when I came out I stopped taking drugs and shortly after that I met your father, Lily, and then we had you. It was a very long time ago now and I never plan to take those kinds of drugs again – ever!'

Lily reached across the table to squeeze her mother's hand.

'That's okay mum. But why are you worried about all that now? I know you won't take them again.'

Sylvia looked tearful. 'I know that too, but unfortunately your father doesn't seem to…' She broke off, unable to finish, and buried her face in the tea towel. Lily felt confused. What had it got to do with her father? They hadn't heard from him in nearly a year. Before he'd left, there'd been years of rows and slamming doors. It had been quite a relief when he'd moved out. On the whole, Lily tried not to think about him too much, particularly the things she missed about him. That way she didn't feel too sad. When he first left, he'd taken Lily out a few times, to the cinema or to the park. But they'd both been a bit shy and awkward with each other. It hadn't been the same as when he'd lived at home. Despite that, she'd been really upset when he broke the news that he was going to live in America.

'I'll get you over for holidays, Lil,' he'd promised.' We'll go to Disneyland together.'

But it had never happened. All she'd got were a few scrawled postcards and then nothing at all. She'd given up being cross and disappointed about it. Anyway, she and Mum were getting on just fine without him. Life was much more peaceful.

'Lily,' Sylvia was able to talk again. 'Your dad has written from the States, he says …' Her voice was thick with tears. 'He says he wants to fight for custody of you. He wants you to go and live with him over there. He says he's been doing really well and now he's settled in a nice house with a pool, he thinks he can give you opportunities there that I can't afford to over here. He says if I don't agree, he'll take it through the courts. If that happens, he'll tell them about the drugs and my going to prison and then he'll be bound to win. You know, Lily, if you really wanted to go I wouldn't stop you, but I hate him threatening us like this.'

Lily's head was a whirl of emotions. Part of her was pleased her dad wanted to see her again, part of her was angry with him, part of her really wanted to live in a house with a pool. But most of her definitely did not want to leave her mum.

'I want to stay with you!' Lily flung herself across the room at her mum and suddenly they were both crying and hugging each other.

Rose didn't know what to think. She didn't want Lily to go to America; they were just getting to know each other. She'd longed for a friend and now, just as she'd found one, she was being taken away. On the other hand, she could see Lily might want to see her father again – and a house with a pool!

Sylvia blew her nose firmly. 'Your dad's coming over to England sometime in the next few weeks, so I'll try and meet with him and see if we can sort this out, without going to court. Until then I don't want either of you to worry too much. We'll try and get on as normal, okay, girls?'

It was hard at first to think of anything else except Sylvia's news, but over the next few days life gradually returned to normal. Strangely enough, just as things at home were getting worse for Lily, things at school were getting better and better. Rose was turning out to be very popular with the other children. They seemed to really like her quaintness and her endless enthusiasm for playground games. Lily found herself included in these more and more and, for the first time, actually enjoyed joining in. This was mainly because Rose was there, but also because she was worrying less about being teased. If Rose could get away with being different, so could she!

Rose was having the time of her life. She'd never had so much fun before. It took her a while to figure out quite what it was about the future that made her feel so much better. Then, one day after school, walking down Whiteladies Road with an ice lolly in one hand and swinging her gym bag in the other, she realised – no one *ever* told her off, or not seriously, not like they really meant it. No one talked about 'God's vengeance on the wicked', no one told her she had to be good all the time. Nobody mentioned death either, which was pretty strange as surely people must still be dying?

She had come to terms with the fact that Sylvia and Lily were heathens. They didn't mind Rose saying her prayers every night and they hadn't tried to convert her. In her old life, Rose had spent a good deal of her time worrying about being a sinner and dying and going to hell. Somehow, in her new life she didn't feel anxious about any of these things. Maybe because no one around her seemed to be worrying about them either?

And there were so many treats to be had every day: lovely puddings at school, a cake or a chocolate bar on the way home, ice-cream! She could read what she liked, when she liked. She could watch the amazing 'telly' thing – although Sylvia had started to limit her to two hours a day as Rose had rapidly become addicted.

They could speak at mealtimes without asking permission and Lily could be really quite rude to Sylvia and her mother didn't bat an eyelid. It was odd. Despite the fact she had to be careful all the time not to give herself away, Rose was feeling – for the first time in her life – really quite relaxed.

But at night, when the wind blew, rattling the bedroom window and keeping Rose awake, she had more worrying thoughts. How *was* Rose Perkins managing in 1898? Was she in any danger? Would she catch diphtheria? Then there was Aubrey, with his pale face and hands on his throat. But Rose couldn't bear to think about that. Sometimes, a thought would come into her head. She knew it was wrong, but it just kept slipping back into her mind… what if I never go back? What if I stay here, in this time, for ever? Who would really miss me? I'm just a nuisance to Mama. Janetta would be sad, but she's got her own family. Aubrey's got his brothers. Oh no! I mustn't think about *them*.

It was a few days after Sylvia's shocking news that Lily reminded Rose they had promised to revisit her house. 'I *do* believe you and everything, but it would still be cool for you to show me some stuff. I've asked Mum and she says she *does* know the woman who owns it and she's sure she wouldn't mind us looking round the house for a school project. That's what I told her we were doing. Its true as well 'cos Miss Wright *has* asked us to write about a Victorian home.'

'All right.' It was funny, but Rose didn't feel nearly as keen to see her old house now as she had when she'd first arrived. Then, her home was still fresh in her mind and she'd longed to see it again – to get away from the strangeness of life in 2008. Now, even though she'd only been with Lily's family just over a week, they seemed far more real and familiar to her than her old life.

As they walked towards Cossins Place, Rose felt a shiver of fear. Time had shifted for her once before. Suppose going into her old house made it shift again? What might happen when she rapped on the old swan knocker? Who would answer the door? Would it be the present-day owner? Or would it be Janetta in her black dress and starched white cap?

They were at the front door. Rose lifted up her arm and fitted the swan's neck into the palm of her hand. Her heart thumping in her chest, she lifted it up and let it bang down against the wood.

Instantly the door swung open. 'Hello girls, I've been expecting you.'

A tall elegant woman in a black turtleneck jumper and jeans stood smiling at the door. She had long brown hair tied back in a loose bun and a beautiful peacock-coloured scarf around her shoulders. Behind her on a green coat rack, Rose could see a jumble of coats and hats – including a knitted orange and purple one that she guessed must have come from Sylvia.

'Come on in, girls. Don't be shy. I'm afraid my two big girls are out, but I've got a few things to show you that I've found around the house, or dug up in the garden. I'm Olivia by the way.'

The girls stepped over the brass step and into the long, high hallway.

'Look at the lovely plaster mouldings round the walls and ceiling.' Olivia pointed upwards at the cracked white decorations that looked like bits of icing off a Christmas cake. 'I *think* they used to be flowers and fruit but they've been painted over so many times they've just turned into blobs.'

'Yes, they *were* fruits and flowers,' blurted out Rose. Then seeing Lily's face, she quickly followed up with, 'We've been learning about Victorian decorations at school.'

Olivia nodded and led them out of the hall into what had been the dining room, the scene of Rose's last sin-filled breakfast. Rose gasped. The dark green wallpaper was gone and the room was now painted a sunny yellow. More importantly, a whole wall was missing and you could see straight through to the kitchen.

'There's not much left here from Victorian times. They would have had a coal- fired range instead of a cooker and no central heating of course. The poor maid would have had to light all the fires every morning.'

It was strange for Rose, hearing her everyday, normal life talked about as if it was ancient history. It was even odder being in her own house in the future. Suppose the ghosts of her mother and Janetta were still here, would she be able to see them? And what about Rose Perkins? Was she here? If she concentrated really hard could she hear a rustle of silk… a banging of copper pots… a child crying?

'Rose, stop looking like a loony!' Lily was prodding her in the side. 'Olivia wants to know if you'd like to see upstairs?'

'Oh yes please!'

Rose followed them up the curved staircase with its walnut handrail, still smooth and cool under her hand. The rooms around her seemed so light and spacious. The bare windows with their simple curtains let the sunshine flood in. Rose realised she had never seen her parents' room in daylight. It had always been a dark, gloomy place overshadowed by two huge, mahogany wardrobes. It had reeked of the bitter smell of naphthalene moth balls. Her mother stuffed them in every drawer to stop them eating her precious wraps and shawls. But the memory Rose could never wipe from her mind was of the morning Janetta led her in to see her father's body, laid out in his best morning suit on the bed, his face grey and cold.

'You're looking like a loony again,' whispered Lily bringing Rose back to the present with a jolt.

Olivia led them into Rose's old room. Lily could see it was a typical teenager's bedroom. Every inch of the floor was covered in clothes, and every inch of the walls was covered in posters and photographs, mainly of other girls sticking their tongues out and pulling faces.

'My bed!' Rose yelled and lifted up a pile of T-shirts to reveal an iron bed post.

Olivia looked surprised. 'You've got one like this at home? This one's an original Victorian one I believe. We bought it off the previous owners – I don't know where they got it from.'

Rose turned and whispered urgently in Lily's ear.

'It *is* my bed. I can prove it to you: the bed knob at the bottom right hand corner will be missing.'

To Olivia's surprise, both girls started rummaging under the duvet that had been flung over the end of the bed.

'Oh dear. Bea is *so* untidy. I'm quite embarrassed to let you see it like this. It really is a lovely bed – it's a shame one of the knob's is missing. I did find an old one when I was digging in the garden. It looked so similar to the ones on the bed I could almost believe it was the missing one but it was too covered in rust to tell for certain.'

Lily unhooked a jumper to reveal the bedstead. Rose grinned triumphantly at her. It was just as she'd said – the bottom right hand knob was missing. Lily stared at the empty space chewing her lower lip thoughtfully. Up until now there had been a niggling doubt in the back of her mind. Had Rose just been making it all up? Maybe she really *was* Rose Perkins and had conjured up the whole time travel business because she was unhappy being so far away from her mum.

Lily had wanted Rose's story to be true, but part of her had also been frightened that it actually might be. So now, looking at the empty space where the bed knob should have been, she began to feel properly scared.

Chapter Nine

Cotham Park Gardens

That night Lily tossed and turned, unable to sleep. If Rose can time, travel does that mean *I* could time travel too? she thought. And how exactly did Rose manage it? She was getting hot with all her churning around in bed, so she tried sticking her feet out from under the covers but that made them too cold. She tried turning her pillow over so the cool side rested against her cheek, but nothing worked. On the other side of the room she could hear Rose rustling and sighing.

Lily sat up. 'I just can't get off to sleep Rose. What do *you* do to help you drop off?'

'I think about galaxies and stars and… er… death.'

'Death!' Lily sat up in bed. 'Why on earth do you do that?'

Rose thought. When her father had died – after the funeral – she'd kept worrying about him alone in that dark, cold coffin under the ground. It had worried her so much she'd even asked her mother about it.

'His mortal body is a mere husk now, Rose. His soul will have ascended into Heaven and Eternal Life.'

Rose was not as comforted by this thought as her mother had hoped. 'But how can he breathe down there?'

'His body no longer needs to breathe. His spirit has gone.'

'What if he opens his eyes and it's all black?'

Mrs Cox was getting impatient. She was worn down with all the burial arrangements and money worries.

'Rose, his body can neither breathe, see, nor hear.'

'Smell?'

'Rose, you are being quite unnecessary!'

Mrs Cox had swept out of the room, leaving Rose to practise plugging her ears, holding her breath and closing her eyes as tightly as she could. After a few seconds she got a bursting sensation in her chest and tiny pinpoint explosions of light behind her eyes. Then a feeling of falling backwards – a little like going off to sleep. If that's what death is like, it's not *so* bad, she thought. And after that, if she was lying awake at night worrying about her father, she would think about the falling backwards feeling and it helped her to fall asleep.

Rose tried to explain this as best she could to Lily. Lily was unconvinced.

'But aren't you *afraid* of dying? I mean it just doesn't seem a very relaxing thing to think about last thing at night.'

'It's not the thinking about death exactly, it's thinking about nothingness and just loads of blackness that sends me off to sleep. I *am* afraid of dying, of course I am. Actually, that's really what brought me here in the first place.'

'What do you mean?' Lily was wide awake now and curious. 'You've never said exactly why you came here. It must have been something really awful to make you want to leave your home and your family and everything.'

Rose closed her eyes and dug her nails into her palms. The truth was, she didn't want to think about it herself, let alone say it out loud to Lily. Saying it out loud made it real and she wanted, more than anything, for it not to be real. She took a deep breath and then told Lily all about that evening: the knocking on the door, cook sobbing, Eustace dying, Aubrey…

Lily was looking at Rose and frowning slightly. Something was niggling away at the back of her mind. She felt that the normally truthful Rose wasn't telling her the whole story. 'I understand why you were so upset – about Aubrey and his little brother I mean – but what I don't understand is why *you* were so worried. Had you been playing with them that day? Did you think you might catch it from them?'

There was another pause and some more throat clearing from Rose. 'I – er – did something that day, something not at all like me. I'm quite ashamed of myself…'

'Oh come on, Rose, you're in modern times now. I promise you I won't be shocked. You've got to get over the table leg thing.'

'Table leg?' Rose was completely taken aback. 'What on earth do table legs have to do with it?'

'We learnt about it at school,' Lily explained patiently. 'The Victorians were so embarrassed about bare legs they even covered up table and piano legs.'

'*Sometimes*,' Rose replied crossly. 'Honestly, the things you learn about us at school are so utterly trivial – like putting little boys up chimneys. That only ever happened in *really* big houses with *really* big chimneys. Our sweep just used ordinary brushes.

Why don't you learn more about the Empire and the Queen? They're *much* more important.'

'Oh Rose, just forget it! Tell me what you did that day. I want to know what you're so embarrassed about.'

Rose thought back. It was only a few weeks ago, but it seemed so far away now – something that had happened in another time, another world…

She spent the morning shopping with Janetta on Chandos Road. Then she had that funny turn in the wool shop and Mrs F gave her the crystal. After that they bumped into Aubrey in the Dairy and he annoyed her by telling her about his new rollerskates – he must have known she couldn't possibly join him in the park and have a go on them. Then it was back home, with a long boring afternoon ahead of her. Normally she would have spent the time reading and sewing with her mother, but that day Mrs Cox was lying down in a darkened room with a damp cloth on her head. The slightest sound aggravated her headache so there was very little that Rose could do.

She decided to pretend she was a detective, hunting a dangerous criminal mastermind. This involved tiptoeing around the house, trying not to be seen by any of the grown ups. Cook and Janetta were very good at pretending not to see her, and then acting really surprised when she jumped out at them.

Unfortunately, on this occasion, Cook was a little too surprised and let out a piercing scream. 'Ye Gods and little fishes! Miss Rose, you'll be the death of me with all your creeping around.'

At that moment Mrs Cox appeared at the door with a thunderous look on her face. 'How many times do I have to tell you to be quiet? I really cannot bear it. Janetta!'

Janetta came into the hallway. She was tying the bow on her best silk bonnet ready to go out. She only had one half day off in the whole week and she had planned a trip to the new 'Tin' church in Westbury – it was made, Rose was amazed to hear, entirely of corrugated iron – *and* she was not going alone. A certain Mr Ernest Tricks, who for the last six months had been sitting next to her at their weekly Bible class, had finally plucked up courage to ask her to accompany him on an afternoon stroll. So, naturally enough, she had invited him to join her on the walk over to Westbury. She had *not* planned for any company.

Mrs Cox ignored Janetta's reluctant expression. 'Janetta, I need you to take Rose out for the afternoon, and please don't return for at least two hours. I need my rest.'

She didn't wait for Janetta's reply, but whisked out of the room leaving Janetta looking grim-faced and disappointed. It was no use protesting. Mrs Cox was well-known for sacking any servant who didn't do exactly what she wanted and Janetta couldn't afford to be dismissed. She had a widowed mother and seven younger brothers and sisters to support in Barrow Gurney. Rose, herself, was secretly pleased not to have a boring afternoon at home, but she could tell how upset Janetta was by the way she laced Rose's boots up far too tightly and slapped her gloves into her hands.

As they marched up Cossins Place, Rose turned to her. 'Really Janetta, I don't mind if you want to go to your church. You can leave me in the park and I'll wait for you there. I'll sit with all the other Nannies and children. I promise I won't run off or get dirty or anything!'

'Oh no, Miss. I couldn't possibly. What *would* the Mistress say? I've said I'll look after you and so I shall.'

'Could we not just pass *by* the park and see if there's anyone there you could trust to take care of me? Please, *please*, Janetta?'

Rose was keen to avoid a long boring sermon and it had crossed her mind that maybe – just maybe – Aubrey, and his rollerskates might be there.

Janetta was wavering. After all she had waited six whole months for Mr Tricks to ask her out. They reached the bottom of the road and turned left along the railway line. Ahead was the new Redland Railway Station, the cream and maroon paint gleaming in the summer sunshine. There was the little ticket office and two waiting rooms, one on either side of the track, and the beautiful arched iron foot-bridge between the two. As they crossed over the bridge, Rose looking longingly up the track – as she always did. It ran straight for a while, then curved right and disappeared out of sight. One day I'll catch a train and never come back, she thought. I'll travel to the other side of the world. I will, I will… Rose closed her eyes and felt the sharp edges of the crystal prick against her fingers.

'Come on, Miss Rose, step sharpish. We'll see who's in the park. But if I'm not satisfied they're proper and respectable you'll stay with me, mind!'

Cotham Park Gardens were laid out on a gently sloping slice of land directly behind the railway station. An avenue of high elm trees bordered one side and, on the other, fields and market gardens stretched into the distance. At the centre of the park was a rose garden with tightly weaving paths and clipped hedges. And there, sitting primly on a bench, were the Misses Axteds from Number 48.

The Misses Axteds ran a small boarding school for young ladies. A serious-looking girl of about thirteen was sitting with them while a younger child – her sister Rose guessed, as they had matching bonnets – was hopping about in front. Janetta approached them and, after a short conversation, beckoned Rose over.

'The Misses Axteds have *very* kindly agreed to keep an eye on you whilst I'm gone. *Please* behave – and no trouble mind!'

Rose nodded and Janetta walked briskly away, turning back a few times to check Rose was still there, before disappearing over the brow of Redland Hill. To tell the truth, the thought of sitting next to Mr Tricks for a whole hour was quite thrilling. Should she start calling him Ernest? No it was too early for that. Maybe next time...

Rose stood stiffly by the Axteds and their pupils. The older child was doing some embroidery and hardly looked up. The younger one stared at her unblinkingly with wide blue eyes. Neither of them said a word.

Rose sighed. This wasn't what she had in mind at all. It was just as bad as being at home. 'Please Ma'am, can I take a walk around the paths? I'm afraid I didn't bring anything to do.'

The older of the two women pursed her lips and frowned. Rose was sure she was about to say no, when the younger one leaned forward and smiled. 'Of course you may, Rose, as long as you don't wander too far. And please don't talk to strangers.'

The little girl jumped up excitedly. 'Oh, please may I go too? *Please*, Miss Axted?' Her large eyes turned pleadingly towards the younger lady, but this time the elder Miss Axted got in first.

'No you may *not*, Edie, you are far too much of a flibbertigibbet. Goodness knows what you might get up to. Now sit down and stop making a spectacle of yourself.'

Rose felt sorry for Edie, who gazed mournfully after Rose as she set off down the path. However it did mean that she could choose exactly where she wanted to go, which wasn't something that happened very often in Rose's life. She wandered along, pausing to look at the milestone that Alderman Cope had placed in front of a spindly-looking oak tree. It was there to mark the Queen's Diamond Jubilee. Nearly the whole of Redland had turned out to watch that day. There'd been a brass band and flags and Janetta had even allowed her an ice-cream. 'Mind you don't drip it on your new pinafore though, or there'll be trouble.'

Rose started to play a game with herself, trying to avoid the cracks in the paving stones and humming happily. *There were two in the bed and the little one said…*

There was a sudden grinding of wheels on stone and, in a whirling blur of arms and legs, Aubrey shot round the corner – bang into Rose.

'Oops, sorry old bean! Just getting the hang of these things.' He lay on his back like an upturned turtle. His feet, with the brand new skates on them, were waving in the air. 'Give us a hand up, there's a good chap.'

He held up his arm, grinning in his usual cheeky way. Rose thought he may have bumped into her on purpose. Now would the Miss Axteds count Aubrey as a stranger? But Aubrey carried on grinning and holding out his hand. In the end, Rose thought it would be rude not to, so she grasped his hand and heaved him to his feet, where he wobbled precariously before grabbing onto her shoulder. Rose was anxious that the Axteds might be looking so she prised his fingers off, but he immediately clung onto her hand.

'Do 'scuse me, I'm not being over familiar. It's just a chap can't quite keep his balance yet.'

Rose looked around. They were a long way from the others and hidden by a privet bush, so she let him hold on. His fingers were surprisingly cool and dry. His face, which was very near hers, was creamy coloured with a light dusting of freckles. His dark hair was damp and sticking slightly to his forehead.

With a sudden movement he wrenched his hand away. 'Right, I'm off for another turn around the park.' And with a clatter of wheels he shot out off.

Rose tried to return to her line game, but it wasn't fun any more. Rose sighed to herself. Why do I always have to play by myself? she wondered. I wish I had brothers and sisters or a best friend. Games are so much better when you've got someone to play them with.

She walked by the Miss Axteds so they'd see she was behaving herself. Edie was still sitting on the bench swinging her legs vigorously and looking longingly at her. Rose knew she'd never be able to persuade the Axteds to change their mind, so she gave the little girl a quick smile and then carried on down to the railway line. Perhaps there would be a train that she could wave her handkerchief at – or was she getting a bit too old for that? All the time she was half listening out for the sound of rattling wheels. She turned to look back at the park, but there was no sign of a boy on a pair of rollerskates. She felt oddly disappointed.

'Hey, Rose! Rose!'

The voice came from above her. She craned her neck up and saw a small figure waving from the iron footbridge by the station. It was Aubrey, the skates now hanging from their straps around his neck.

'I couldn't skate on those bumpy stones in the park, but I've found a super place behind the station where you can really whiz about. Come and see! I'll give you a go if you promise not to be a sissy and cry if you fall over.'

Rose knew that she mustn't go. She'd promised Janetta to stay in the park. She'd told the Axteds she'd stay close by. It would most definitely be a sin. But on the other hand she would be very *close* to the park, and Janetta wouldn't be back for ages, and she *so* wanted to have a go on those skates. When she was grown up there'd be loads of time to be really, *really* good…

All the time she was thinking this, she was walking over to the park gate, pushing it open and climbing up the steps of the footbridge. She met Aubrey at the top.

He looked surprised. 'Didn't think you had the pluck old thing, thought you were tied to the old battle-Axted's apron strings!'

'Is that what you call them – the battle-Axteds?'

'Yep, Neville made it up. He's really good at nicknames.'

'Really? What's yours?'

But Aubrey had turned away abruptly and started to race down the steps towards the station. 'Come on if you want a go. Let's get on with it!'

'Wow! That was brave. Weren't you scared you'd get caught?' Lily was sitting on the edge of her bed, looking impressed.

Rose thought. 'No. Because at that moment I wanted to roller-skate more than anything else in the world. So I just did it.'

CHAPTER TEN

Redland Station

There were no trains running and the station waiting rooms were deserted. Aubrey disappeared around the corner of the ticket office and Rose had to run to keep up with him. She wasn't used to running and arrived, puffed and out of breath, at a flat, dusty area behind the station buildings.

'A perfect skating rink!' Aubrey flung out his arms as though he had created it himself. He quickly buckled on his skates. 'I'll do a few turns, then you can have a go.'

Rose felt a bit awkward, standing there watching him swoop around, his arms outstretched like a seagull, that silly grin on his face – but it was worth it to get a go herself. Me, Rose Cox! Rollerskating! It must be like flying, she thought.

A rasping, coughing sound brought her back from her day dreams. Aubrey was doubled over, clutching at his throat. His face was sweaty and red as he stumbled over to Rose. 'Help me get these off, there's a sport. I think I need to give it a rest for a bit. Time for your go!'

The fastenings were awkward and Rose had to wrestle the skates off Aubrey's boots. Then she sat down on a pile of railway sleepers with her feet stuck out in front of her. Aubrey's breathing had returned to normal now and he set to work buckling the skates on to Rose's feet. As he worked he whistled through his teeth. *'Oh my darling, Oh my darling, Oh my darling Clementine! Thou art lost and gone forever, Oh my darling Clementine!'*

A sudden, soft breeze blew across the yard and a blackbird sang. Rose felt a warm rush of happiness so overwhelming that tears pricked at the back of her eyes. I'll never forget this moment, she thought, not as long as I live.

Rose was terrible at rollerskating. One leg went in one direction and one shot off in the other. She could only balance if she took tiny steps forward.

'That's not skating Rose, that's *walking*!' Aubrey teased her.

If he held her hands and walked backwards, she could just about roll along – but whenever she went over an uneven patch it made her giggle and lurch forwards. Aubrey was shaking his head and laughing at her.

'You're a hopeless case, chum. Tell you what – I've got some penny chews, let's stop for a bit and eat them. Then you can have another try.'

They sat on the wooden sleepers and chatted. Rose couldn't say about what. Talking with Aubrey was like that. You never had to *think* what to say next. It was easy. You just said stuff and he said stuff back. And yet you could spend hours doing it and never feel bored. Rose didn't know anyone else she could talk with like that.

'Oh my goodness! Look at the time!' Rose had glanced up at the station clock. Its hands were set at half past three, she'd been in the yard with Aubrey for over an hour. She wrenched the skates off and started to run for the railway bridge.

'Wait, don't run off like that! Wait Rose!'

Aubrey caught up with her just as she reached the gate back into the park, the high laurel hedge hiding them from the gardens beyond.

Rose turned just as Aubrey reached her and they bumped awkwardly together. Then, before Rose had time to think, he'd leant in towards her and brushed his lips over hers. His lips were warm and slightly wet. Rose felt a shock – like electricity – jump through her. She broke away, anxiously looking around to check if anyone had seen them, but the deep green of the laurel had protected them.

Aubrey was standing back looking sheepish. 'I say Rose, I'm most awfully sorry. Swear you won't tell anyone?'

He bit his lower lip and Rose could see a crimson blush creeping up his neck and turning his pale freckled face pink.

Rose found herself smiling. 'I won't, if you won't. Look I really have to go. I'm going to be in heaps of trouble as it is. It's probably best if you stay here until I'm back inside the park. If the battle-axes see me with you they'll be bound to tell my mother – and then I'll never be allowed out *ever* again!' Rose turned and pushed open the wooden gate.

Aubrey called after her, 'If you *are* allowed out again, will you come back to the park sometime? I could teach you how to skate properly then.'

'I *would* like to, but I dare say I won't be allowed out of Janetta's sight and you know she wouldn't approve of me rollerskating – especially with you.'

The gate swung closed behind her and there was no reply from behind the dark green wall of laurel.

'And that was the last time I saw Aubrey.' Rose's voice was flat and sad.

Lily bounced up and down on her bed. 'Come on Rose! What happened next? You can't stop there!'

'Well, there isn't much more to tell. The Axteds had sent the older girl to look for me and they were quite cross that I'd gone out of sight. I told them – and it was true really – that I'd gone to look at the trains. Then the older girl came back and said she hadn't seen me *anywhere* in the park. And she was looking at me rather strangely, which made me think she might have seen me with Aubrey. So I gave her a fierce look and she didn't say any more. Just then Janetta came back. She looked a bit pink and kept apologising for being so late. The Axteds asked how the sermon was and Janetta said that she and Mr Tricks had been so moved by the vicar's talk about the African Missions that they'd given two whole shillings for the collection. Then the younger Miss Axted asked if they would be hearing more of Mr Tricks and then Janetta went really red!'

'I was hoping the Miss Axteds wouldn't tell her they'd lost me, but they did of course and Janetta was furious. She made me apologise to them loads of times and said she was definitely going to tell my mother. That's when I committed my next mortal sin.'

Lily was sitting on the edge of her bed now. 'So what was your first one? Nothing you've said so far has been that bad!'

Rose was glad it was too dark for Lily to see her face. '*You know* – kissing! Kissing Aubrey!'

Lily frowned. 'I don't really know what a mortal sin is, but it must be worse than kissing. Maybe murdering someone or setting fire to their house, but not just *kissing*!'

'Well, it was in *my* time.' Rose felt a bit cross that Lily wasn't taking her seriously. 'Have you ever kissed a boy then?'

'*No*! All boys are yuck! Wasn't it horrible kissing Aubrey?'

Rose thought about it: it had been surprising, unexpected and a bit embarrassing, but no, not actually 'yucky'. 'Well, I wouldn't ever kiss him again of course, even if he were to ask me to. You see, in my time adults were very strict about boys and girls kissing. It's not like now.'

'It's funny, isn't it?' mused Lily. 'In Victorian times you couldn't – but you did and in modern times, I could – but I wouldn't.' Lily remembered about the second mortal sin: 'What was it, Rose? If it's anything like the last one I won't be that shocked.'

Rose heaved a sigh and told her...

Janetta had marched her back to Cossins Place with dire threats to tell her mother how disobedient she had been. Rose could imagine what Mrs Cox's punishments would be:

– Bed at 6pm every evening.

– *No* puddings for a month.

– *No* reading *The People's Friend Annual* on Sundays.

– Writing out at least ten of the Psalms in her best handwriting.

– And definitely, *definitely* no more unaccompanied visits to the park!

Janetta was lifting up her hand to the swan knocker when Rose suddenly reached up and grabbed her arm. 'Did you enjoy the church service Janetta?'

Janetta looked down, surprised. 'What did you say, Miss?'

Rose took a deep breath. 'I just wondered whether you and your friend – what was his name, Mr Tricks? – enjoyed yourselves whilst you left me alone in the park? I was just thinking that Mother might be quite interested to hear about that, mightn't she?'

And that was when Janetta looked down at her, her eyes filled with sadness and dislike. 'Well, Miss Rose! Well really! And it was your suggestion in the first place that I left you there. I would never have thought it of you. You've always been a bit of an odd one mind, but I always thought…'

She stopped and Rose was horrified to see she was starting to cry. 'Oh please, Janetta, I'm sorry, I'm really, *really* sorry. I won't tell Mother – of course I won't!'

Rose felt wretched. Of all the people in the house, she liked Janetta the best. She was the one who stayed up with her when she was sick, who put cool flannels on her forehead and dabbed her pillow with lavender. She was the one who smuggled bread and honey to her when her mother had sent her to bed without any supper and told her those silly jokes she'd got from her younger brothers. And now Rose'd threatened to tell on her to her mother, who would almost certainly sack her if she found out Janetta had left Rose and gone off with a young man.

'Please, Janetta. I'm so very sorry for mentioning Mr Tricks. I won't tell Mama and I don't mind if you tell her I ran off in the park. I shouldn't have done it. It was very wrong of me.'

Of course Rose *did* mind, very much, but she minded even more that Janetta didn't like her.

Janetta's expression seemed to soften slightly. 'Well, Miss Rose,

I think that both you and I have been led into temptation. The devil is always there, waiting for our flesh to be weakened by the lure of Mammon.'

Rose was not at all sure she understood Janetta but she nodded her head solemnly.

Janetta continued, 'I think what you and I must do is to pray to God for forgiveness. I believe there is a six o'clock service at St Saviours. I shall ask your Mother if we can attend and we will pray together for his mercy.' Janetta nodded her head in a satisfied way. 'I do believe this is a matter between ourselves and Our Lord, Miss Rose. No more need be said about it.'

Janetta turned back to the front door and rapped the knocker firmly.

'So that's it? You nearly got in trouble, but then you didn't?'

'Well, yes, but it's the betraying bit that was so awful. That I would have betrayed Janetta to my mother, when really she was the nearest thing to a best friend that I had.'

'So that was another reason you were feeling so horrible that night?'

Rose nodded.

'Tell me more about that old lady – and the wool shop and how exactly you managed to travel in time.'

Rose tried. She explained as much as she could about Mrs F and the crystal and the night when she'd wished so hard to escape. It was difficult to remember the exact words she'd used, but what she did remember was the overwhelming feeling of terror and how frightened she'd been that she'd die too.

'And that's when you held the crystal and wished, like Mrs F told you to?'

Rose nodded, then took a deep breath before speaking again. 'I think I've done a really terrible thing – I've saved myself but think I've killed Rose Perkins!'

She waited ages for Lily to say something. Then she realised there was stifled giggling coming from Lily's bed.

'Rose, you're such a drama queen! How could you have murdered Rose Perkins?'

'I don't mean me *personally* killing her. I mean I've put her in danger – in a situation where *she* might die instead of *me*.'

'How do you mean?'

'It's not something I've done. Its something I didn't do. I didn't think when I wished to be somewhere else that another person would have to take my place. I didn't even wish to travel in time; I just wanted to get away from all the sickness and dying. I wanted to escape. I didn't want to be 'me' anymore!'

'But you are still 'you', aren't you?' Lily asked awkwardly.

'Yes, I think so. Although I'm much braver than I was in my own time. I've done things here I would never have dreamed of doing back home. You know in the playground I went up and talked to all those kids that I'd never met before? I would never have had the chance to do that in my old life. I always used to do exactly what people told me to – although I didn't on that last day of course. I disobeyed Mama and Janetta *and* the Misses Axteds. Oh Lily, I'm just like a murderer!'

Lily had come over and put her arm around Rose's shoulders.

Rose was sobbing quietly. She gulped back her tears and tried to talk again. 'Don't you see? *I'm* alright. I don't seem to have got the diphtheria, but I sent Rose Perkins back. She probably even woke up in my bed. She's surrounded by the illness.

Suppose she dies instead of me?'

CHAPTER ELEVEN

Aubrey's Head

Sylvia was standing at the sink slicing up a mound of vegetables. Beside her were some crisp yellow sticks. Rose had learned that you could boil these up and they became the rubbery strands that Lily and her Mum called 'pasta'. Sylvia cooked an awful lot of pasta, as well as piles of chewy brown rice that reminded Rose unpleasantly of tapioca pudding. Rose stoically ate everything that was put in front of her. She'd had years of being told: 'Eat up! There's poor children in Africa who would give their eye teeth for that.' She'd spent endless mealtimes passing pieces of gristle from one side of her mouth to the other, trying again and again to swallow it, so she could finally be allowed to 'get down'. Sylvia, of course, would never dream of forcing her to eat anything and there was something else about the Staveleys: they were vegetarian.

'Is meat too expensive for you to buy?' Rose had asked Lily after yet another lentil bake supper. 'Or is it your religion...?' She'd trailed off feeling a bit embarrassed.

'No, silly!' Lily had gone into a long and gory explanation about the horrors of killing animals. It left Rose feeling like a mass murderer for ever having enjoyed a slice of bacon.

Over at the sink, Sylvia let out a deep sigh as she hacked at a piece of broccoli. Rose could see her shoulders were hunched and tense.

'Can I help lay the table?' she asked.

'Oh, Rose, darling, you are *so* helpful. Next time I talk to your mum I'm going to tell her what a fantastic job she's done, bringing you up.' Sylvia looked sadly down at her knife. 'Which is more than Mark would say about me.'

Mark, Rose knew, was Lily's dad. And he didn't sound at all like her own dear Papa. When Lily and Sylvia talked about Mark he always sounded cross and grumpy. And then there was that awful thing he'd said about Sylvia not being 'a fit mother', which was obviously untrue.

'Rose, I don't want to scare you, but I am worried that Mark might do something silly while he's over here, like try to snatch Lily and take her back with him to America. I've never told Lily, but he has threatened to do it before. I shouldn't ask you, I know, you're just a child, but could you possibly keep an eye out for anyone strange talking to Lily, or hanging round the school gates. Look, here's a photo of him. He's a bit older and fatter than this now, but you should a be able to recognise him.'

The crumpled picture showed a tall man with longish, fair hair which flopped over his face as he laughed back at the camera. He was holding a plump baby in a red spotty swim suit, with a cloud of auburn curls. He didn't look cross or grumpy.

'Is that Lily?' Rose pointed at the child.

Sylvia didn't answer immediately. She was staring at the man in the photo with a sad, almost longing expression. Rose felt surprised. Grown-ups were really hard to understand sometimes.

'Yes, yes, that's Lily. What a lovely roly-poly baby she was. Now if you could keep a look out for me that would be great. I don't want to scare Lily, so could you keep this just between ourselves?'

But Rose wasn't listening. She was still staring at the photo, and most particularly at Baby Lily.

'What's that in her hand?' she asked, although she was pretty sure she knew already what the answer would be.

'Oh that – that's an old bit of crystal. Not really the most suitable toy for a baby, but Lily loved it. I think it was the way it caught the light.'

'Where did you get it from?' Rose thought she knew the answer to this question as well, but she needed to be sure.

'It was from the old lady who runs the wool shop. Did you know that your mother and I lived round here, years ago, when we were students? The old woman gave it to me when I was in there buying wool. She said it would come in useful one day and I suppose it did – as a toy for Lily!'

'Do you still have it?' Rose hardly dared ask, in case Sylvia said it had been lost or broken.

'Yes, I keep it in a box on the mantelpiece, to remind me of when Lily was little. Is everything going all right for you, Rose? Are you settling in okay? I've been so caught up with things I haven't had time to ask how you are.'

'Oh, I'm very well. Thank you for asking.' Rose's head was whirling with thoughts of the crystal and Mrs F, but then she remembered there was something she really needed an answer to.

'Mrs Staveley – I mean Sylvia – could I ask you something?'

'Fire away, sweetie.'

'Well, um, someone at school has got… er…' Rose swallowed, feeling guilty about telling a white lie. 'They've got, um, *diphtheria*, and we were wondering how you catch it. I mean, if you say…' Rose was blushing furiously now. 'Kissed someone, would that mean you'd get it? And how long would it take to get ill? And if you were ill, would you definitely die? And, if you didn't die, could you cure it?' Rose stopped gabbling and took a deep breath.

Sylvia was looking horrified. 'Diphtheria! *Diphtheria*! Are you sure that's what they've got?'

Rose nodded emphatically.

'Well, good heavens. I'm very surprised the school hasn't sent a note round.'

'It only just happened,' put in Rose.

'Oh, I see. Well it's very unusual nowadays, because everyone gets vaccinated when they're a baby, which means you can't catch it. You'll be fine, Rose. I know Caroline made sure you had all your injections before she took you off travelling. And anyway, I'm sure it can be treated now. As for kissing, I'm really not sure, I don't suppose you'd always catch it that way. If it would make you feel better I'll contact the school and ask them for more information…'

'Oh no, please don't do that! Lily and I were just curious, that's all.'

Luckily, just at that moment the phone rang, which distracted Sylvia from asking any more about it.

Rose was dying to tell Lily what she'd discovered about diphtheria but she had to wait until Lily got back from her karate class. At last she heard the front door bang. She raced down to the sitting room where she found Lily lolling over a bean bag dressed in a white Japanese-style costume.

'What *is* karate?' asked Rose. 'Is it to do with carrots? Is it a vegetarian thing?'

Lily snorted with laughter. 'No it's nothing to do with vegetables! Karate is, well, kind of organised fighting.'

'Fighting! For girls!'

'Girls can do anything they want nowadays. You can be an astronaut, fireman, prime-minister. Yeah, really!' Lily could see Rose didn't believe that last one.

Rose lowered her voice to a hushed whisper. 'Lily, I've found out something really important from your mum about diphtheria. *You* can't get it cos you've had a vaxi-something and neither can Rose Perkins, 'cos she's had hers too!'

Lily sat up grinning. 'That's brilliant news isn't it? You haven't killed her after all. In fact, she's probably having a wonderful adventure, just like you!'

'Hmm… 'Rose wasn't so sure about the last bit. Lessons with her mother and visits to church with Janetta might not be a 21st century child's idea of a good time. 'I still don't know if I'll get diphtheria, but it doesn't seem likely now. I feel fine and its ages since Aubrey kissed me. But even if I did, your mum says they can cure it now.' Rose shivered. 'It doesn't make me want to rush back to my own time, though. I feel much safer here.'

'And I don't want you to go either. But I suppose you'll have to swap back when Rose Perkins' mum gets better – so she can go back to Peru. Won't you?'

Rose nodded, but a small voice was nagging away at the back

of her mind. 'Do you? Do you have to go back? You could see Peru. You could be safe forever from all those awful diseases that they can cure now in their shiny, new hospitals.' Maybe she could fool Caroline into thinking she really was her daughter? After all, Sylvia hadn't guessed – and she'd picked up the real Rose Perkins from the airport.

'Lily, has your mum ever said I look different – you know, from when she saw me at the airport?'

'Nope. She said you slept all the way here on the backseat. And any way Mum's not the best at noticing people's appearance – look at her hats!'

Rose was thinking. *Actually that first morning when I came down to breakfast, she did look hard at me. She said something about not having realised how like Caroline I looked. That's strange… that I should look like Caroline, I mean.*

'Not as strange as your Mrs F and the crystal and the time-travelling!' Lily turned around to look at Rose. 'You do still have the crystal don't you?'

Rose nodded. She'd hidden it under the bed wrapped up in one of Sylvia's woolly hats.

'I really don't want you to go. It's been brilliant having you here,' Lily turned over on her stomach and started picking at the carpet. She looked sad.

'So you don't think I'm peculiar then, or old fashioned?' Rose asked.

'Well, I did a bit that first day when you wouldn't say anything and you looked like a loony all the time, before you told me about the time travel. But now I think you're brilliant. I'm going to miss you loads when you go.'

'Really?' Rose felt a happy, warm glow. *I never want to feel lonely again,* she thought. *I never want to go back to how things were.*

Sylvia called them through for their cabbage *au gratin* and then they played next door with Freddy and Ellie, the Doctor's children. Freddy was really annoying and kept pushing the girls off the trampoline, so in the end they hopped back over the garden wall and watched telly till bedtime.

Exhausted from all the karate and trampolining, Lily fell asleep immediately. Rose tossed and turned and put a pillow over her head to drown out the noise of Lily's snoring. Outside the rain and wind added to the din and she thought she heard branches scraping along the glass. But that couldn't be- there were no trees outside Lily's window.

Rose started to dream of Reverend Sylvester leaning over his pulpit in his long black surplus. He was staring straight at her and, as he leant towards her, his body seemed to writhe and lengthen until he'd stretched into a long, black snake, his head shrunk down to two yellow eyes. He started to coil around her neck so she could hardly breathe. Frantically she tried to shout, *One… two… three… wake up! One… two… three… wake up!* just like her cousins had taught her to do if she had a bad dream. But she couldn't squeeze out a single word as the coils strangled around her throat.

She awoke. She was lying flat on her back on a soft, white-sheeted mattress. She wasn't in Lily's room and it wasn't her bed at home. She had a strong impression of someone lying beside her, breathing in a stuttery, gasping kind of way. Rose felt a rising panic. Where was she? Who was that beside her? She tried to turn her head but it felt like it was made of lead. No matter how hard she tried, she couldn't move it an inch. The desperate breathing was getting louder and from somewhere else in the room she could hear hushed voices murmuring. She tried again to move. Nothing. She was completely paralysed.

A deep male voice was talking. 'The next few days are critical. Keep him comfortable and try to get his temperature down. We'll move him to the fever hospital first thing in the morning.'

Rose knew that voice. It was Dr Ormorod, her family doctor. But what was he doing here?

A female voice came from close by the bed. 'Please be well, darling. Please try to be well!'

A hand appeared above Rose's head, holding a cool, damp cloth. It reached down and placed the flannel on *her* forehead. It was then Rose realised – the breathing wasn't coming from besides her. It *was* her.

Something was very, very wrong. She strained again to move her leaden muscles, but she was trapped inside a completely unresponsive body… and she knew now exactly where she was, and that she was dying.

'Aubrey! Aubrey!' she called out to him in her mind. 'Aubrey, you've got to let me go. I'm trapped in your head!' There was no answer, just the awful breathing. 'Aubrey let me out, help me, please! If you don't let me out I might die with you.' The stuttering gasps continued. 'Aubrey, I'm going to come back and get you, I promise. I'm sorry I didn't come sooner. I'm really sorry. I was having such a good time and I forgot all about my promise to Mrs F. I think I know how to save you, Aubrey, but you have to let me go back so I can sort things out. I don't know if you can hear me, but if you can, let me go – now!'

There was a very faint change in the breaths and the woman's voice came again. 'He seems a little calmer now, Doctor. I'll start to pack his things.' Her hand dabbed at Aubrey's forehead again. 'Don't worry sweetheart, I'll bring your lucky crystal.' She turned back towards the Doctor. 'That strange old lady in the wool shop gave it to him, the morning he got ill. He's been clutching it ever since. She told him it would bring good luck, although I can't say it has done so, so far.'

Rose was certain now what she had to do.

'Aubrey, if you can hear me, listen very carefully. When they come to take you to the fever hospital I want you to hold on to the crystal and wish very, *very* hard. It's really important you do this. Please try to give me a sign you've understood.'

Rose felt a strange tingling sensation where her hand should have been. Then she realised she could feel a sharp lump in the palm of her hand – it was the crystal. Aubrey *had* heard her, she was sure of it.

'I'm coming to save you, Aubrey. I'm coming very soon and I'm not going to let you die!'

Chapter Twelve

The Time Wish

Rose was trying to shake Lily awake.

Lily lay deep under her bed clothes. All that was visible were a few strands of red hair. 'I'm asleep. Leave me alone!' she moaned, curling even tighter into a ball.

'No, Lily, this is really important. I'm not joking! You can't go back to sleep now.' Rose put her head close to where she guessed Lily's ear must be. 'It's life or death!' she hissed, not wanting to wake Sylvia up by shouting too loudly.

'Oh, urgh, okay.' Lily struggled up reluctantly, rubbing her eyes, her face all creased from sleep. 'Whose life? Whose death then?'

'Aubrey's.' Rose explained what had happened.

'Sounds like a bad dream to me,' said Lily. She didn't sound convinced. 'I get those dreams where you can't move all the time.'

'No, this was different. You've got to believe me, Lily. I've been really wicked, forgetting about Aubrey and my promise to Mrs F. After all, she saved my life and now I've got to save Aubrey's. I've got to get him to this time, so he can be cured.'

Lily thought for a moment. 'Although when you were in the

wool shop you didn't know exactly what you were promising, which isn't really fair is it? And you might not have died if you'd stayed in your own time, so you can't be sure she saved your life, can you?'

Rose thought for a moment. 'I made a promise and I'm going to keep it. It's important to keep your promises to people.'

Lily nodded. 'Okay, so what are you going to do about it at' – she peered at her watch – 'five o'clock in the morning?'

'We're going to the wool shop.'

Lily looked incredulous. 'Now? Have you gone bonkers? There's no way it would be open at this time in the morning.'

They left a note for Sylvia:

> *Dear Mum, gone for a jog. Back soon. Don't worry.*
> *Love you lots.*
> *Lily*
> *XXXXXXX*

Rose thought it was probably a mistake to have said 'Don't worry', because that was exactly the kind of thing that did make adults worry. But then again they could hardly have written, 'Gone time travelling, may not be back this century.'

'Brrhh! I wish I'd brought my coat.' Lily hunched her shoulders up against the surprisingly chilly air. There was a pale pink light as the sun rose over the railway line and the street lights were just beginning to dim and fade. Most of the houses were still blank-faced, curtains drawn, but there was a light on in the bakery and the delicious, doughy smell of baking bread. Rose was striding ahead, seemingly quite unafraid to be walking around the city at dawn. Lily followed a little more nervously, ready to practise karate chops on anyone who jumped out at them. Nobody did, and soon they were standing in the glass-panelled porch of the wool shop. Rose stared up at the writing. It promised 'Personal Service' and 'Experienced Attention' – just like in her own time. She felt instantly comforted and at home. From far at the back of the shop a faint light flickered.

'She's there!' breathed Rose and put her hand up to push open the door.

As the familiar tinkle of the bell rang out, the hunched form by the fire turned round to smile at them. 'Welcome, little Rose, welcome. And I see you have brought the other little flower with you. Good. Very, very good. We will need you both.'

Lily stood trembling in the doorway. Where were Maureen and Michelle? The two sisters had run the wool shop for as long as she could remember. She'd never seen this old woman before. Her hair was full of clips and ribbons and her long orange skirts were covered in mirrors. Rose had rushed over and knelt down in front of her.

'It was you! It was you up on the Downs. I didn't recognise you – you looked younger and your voice was different. I'm so sorry Mrs F. You tried to remind me about Aubrey and I didn't take any notice. I was too busy having fun.'

'Hush now, Rose. You're here now – and we don't have much time.'

'Where's Maureen? Where's Michelle?' Lily burst in. Mrs F smiled and rocked her chair.

'They have been very good, looking after my shop for me.

126

I can't be here all the time you see.'

'But you said this was your dream – that you'd always wanted your own wool shop,' interrupted Rose accusingly.

Mrs F nodded. 'There are different dreams, Rose, for different times.'

'So your tent's your dream now?'

The old woman nodded again. 'My tent – my freedom to go anywhere in the world I choose.'

'And how come you're getting younger not older each time I see you?'

Mrs F held up her hand. 'Don't try and understand too much, Rose. What is important is saving Aubrey, that's all you must think about now.'

'But Rose Perkins – is she alright? Please tell me!' Rose pleaded.

'She is fine, my child. I would not have put her in any danger. Let us just say she is having her own adventure- and all will be well in the end.'

Rose opened her mouth to ask another question but Mrs F shook her head and pointed at the face of the carriage clock standing on the mantelpiece. 'No more questions, Rose. It's nearly six o'clock and I think you both know what you must do.'

'I know to hold the crystal and I know to wish but I don't know where to do it. Do we have to go back to my bedroom?' Rose looked worried.

'Exactly! There you see, you do know what to do,' Mrs F stood up, her stiff petticoats rustling, and fished inside a china vase for a large brass key. 'This is the key for Number 12 Cossins Place. Maureen has it so she can feed their cat when they're away.' She looked hard at Rose. 'You must post it back through the letterbox when you return.'

'I will,' agreed Lily, although Mrs F had not been looking at her.

Lily was glad to get out of the wool shop. She couldn't quite believe she'd really met Rose's mysterious Mrs F. But could it all still be a huge trick? Dreamt up by Rose and the old lady? Part of her still found the whole time travel story just too bizarre. No matter how much she liked Rose, could she really believe her? Well, if I see her disappear in front of my eyes I'll have to, she thought. Where was Rose anyway? Lily peered back into the dimly lit shop. She could see Rose and Mrs F talking. Rose seemed to be showing her something. What were they doing?

Rose came racing out of the shop. Lily started to ask what had happened, but Rose dragged her off up the street. 'No time to talk now, we're late!'

They ran all the way up Fairview Drive and on to Cossins Place. Then they stopped, breathless, in front of Number 12. Rose took out the front door key but Lily grabbed her arm, suddenly feeling very anxious.

'Rose, we can't just go in there. They'll think we're burglars. We'll get arrested!'

Rose turned to Lily, her face full of certainty. 'There's no choice, Lily. We *have* to do this or Aubrey will die.'

She slid the key into the lock and turned it, then carefully pushed open the door. They tiptoed over the soft oriental rug in the hallway.

So far so good thought Lily, but her stomach was churning with fear.

'Miaooow!' A high pitched mewing and scratching came from behind the kitchen door. Lily went rigid, her eyes widened with terror. She mouthed at Rose. 'What shall we do?'

Rose thought for a second and then opened the kitchen door. A startled grey cat stared unblinkingly at them, then shot across the hall, slid around the front door and out into the night. Both girls stood trembling and staring up the curved stairway to the landing above, but no sound came down from the bedrooms. They had got away with it. Rose led the way up the stairs. She knew every creaky step from her detective games, and she signalled to Lily to follow her footsteps exactly.

Lily's heart was beating horribly loudly against her chest. She couldn't believe Rose had talked her into this. Maybe it was a dream… maybe she was actually safe and warm and curled up in her own bed? She tried closing her eyes and opening them again. No, she was still in the strange hallway. They crept the last few steps onto the landing. Rose's bedroom door stood slightly ajar. Rose's stomach gave a lurch. Suppose there was someone sleeping in there? She peered around the door and gave a sigh of relief. The room was still piled up with clothes and teenage mess, but the bed was stripped and empty.

'It's alright,' she mouthed back at Lily and beckoned her in. They pushed the door closed behind them and waited for their eyes to get used to the gloom. Lily felt calmer now. After all, they'd made it to the bedroom without getting caught. She tried to put the thought of the return journey out of her mind. She turned to

Rose. 'Do you want me to sit with you while you wish?'

Lily felt suddenly very sad. This morning's adventure had happened so quickly, she'd barely had time to think about how much she would miss Rose. Would she ever see her again? It was so strange to think Rose was going back to live her whole life, a life that would be over and done with before Lily would even be born.

Her eyes started to fill up with tears and she leaned forward to give Rose a last hug. It was then that she noticed Rose was staring at her with a strange, intense expression on her face.

'What is it? Why are you looking at me like that, Rose?' She drew back. Something was wrong, something wasn't going to plan.

'I'm not going, Lily,' said Rose. She spoke very slowly and deliberately. 'You are.'

Lily gasped aloud. 'I can't! What about my mum? She'd be so worried, I just can't leave!'

Rose grabbed her hand urgently. 'She's worried already. She thinks your dad is going to kidnap you and take you back to America. You'll be better off back in my time for a bit. You're probably safer there than here.'

'What?' Lily looked amazed. 'Are you sure she said that – you're not just telling me to persuade me to go back?'

'No, it's true. Honestly. Although I really want you to save Aubrey as well.'

'But I don't even know what he looks like!' Lily was feeling increasingly desperate. This was not what she'd been expecting at all.

'You don't have to,' Rose explained patiently. 'You won't even see him. You see you'll swap places with him, just like I did with

Rose Perkins.'

'You mean I'll turn into a boy?' Lily was horrified – and also just a bit curious. What would *that* be like?

'No! You swap time, not bodies. And Mrs F will make sure you get back safely when the time's right. She promised me.' Rose looked at Lily with her dark pleading eyes. 'Please do it, Lily, please! I need to get Aubrey treated as quickly as possible. As soon as he's better you can come home – cross my heart and hope to die.' Rose traced a cross on her chest, just like she used to do with her cousins when they had important promises to keep.

Lily's mouth was dry with fear and excitement. She wanted an adventure and she'd always longed to travel in time, but now there was actually a chance to do it she wasn't sure she was brave enough. It's a bit like jumping off the highest diving board at the swimming pool, she thought. You think you can't and then suddenly you do. You just step out into the air and fall and fall…

'Yes! Yes! I'll do it,' she blurted, jumping up onto the bed. 'But I've got to do it now, quickly, before I change my mind. Where's the crystal?'

Rose reached into her pocket. When she uncurled her hand there was not one, but two jagged pieces of glass lying in her palm.

'But that's my special glass!' Lily pointed at the second piece in Rose's hand. 'I had that when I was a baby. Was this what you were showing Mrs F?'

Rose nodded. She held them up and briefly locked them together. They fitted perfectly to form half of a sphere, leaving one side rough where the two remaining pieces had shattered off.

'Rose Perkins has one – Mrs F told me- and so does Aubrey.

Mrs F gave it to him the day we went rollerskating. I told him to wish with it when he's on his way to the fever hospital,' Rose looked worriedly at her watch. 'It's nearly six-thirty. We've got to do it now or they'll start to wake up and find us here. Are you ready, Lily?'

Lily nodded and Rose handed her the crystal. It felt very cool and heavy in her palm. She crushed her fingers around it, the sharp edges digging into her flesh.

'Now? Shall I wish now? And what shall I wish for?'

Rose thought hard and then answered, 'You have to wish to travel back and save Aubrey. You've got to put all your will into wanting it more than anything else in the world. That's what I did.'

Rose stood with her back to the window. Outside the sun was rising above the copper beech tree. She could see Lily quite clearly: she was sitting on the bed with her eyes closed and her fists clenched. Suddenly her eyes snapped open and she stared straight at Rose.

'I'll try and find a way of contacting you while I'm there. I'll bury a message in the park, under the milestone tree. Look for it Rose... please...'

Something odd was happening as Lily was speaking. It was if the sun had gone behind a cloud and she was becoming greyer, less distinct. Rose could still make out her outline, but not her face. Rose glanced down at her watch: six-thirty exactly. She looked up. Nothing. The bed was empty. Even though she had known it was going to happen, Rose couldn't quite believe it. She ran to the bed. There was just a slight dip in the mattress where Lily had been sitting only a few seconds before. Rose looked around the room. It was completely empty and the door was still firmly shut. Lily had vanished into thin air.

Rose was suddenly acutely aware of being all alone in a house that was both familiar and yet very strange. She was also far from her own time and with no one now to share her secret with – no one except Aubrey. Aubrey! Of course he must be here somewhere. If Mrs F was right he should have swapped places with Lily. But where on earth was he? She crept out onto the landing. She should be able to hear his ragged breathing if he was in the house. She listened carefully but all she could hear were the whispery creaks of the house settling around her and a few early morning birds. She just knew he wasn't here. If he'd been near, she would have felt it.

She tiptoed carefully back into the hallway and gently opened the front door. A ball of grey fur pelted by her and straight up the stairs meowing loudly. Oh no! She heard a door burst open upstairs and her heart started to hammer wildly. She couldn't afford to be caught now. She ran out of the door, slamming it shut behind her. No time to stop and lock it. Rose ran all the way to the wool shop, not daring to look behind her, and threw herself into the porch, pressing herself up against glass panel of 'Personal Service'. There were no footsteps behind her, no shouting of 'Stop, thief!'

As her breathing gradually returned to normal she turned and peered through the window. It was completely dark, no firelight flickering, no outline of an old woman rocking. Rose tried the door. It wouldn't open. She shook it back and forth but it was firmly locked. Then to her horror a terrific clanging broke out directly above her head – a burglar alarm!

She shoved the key through the letterbox and ran off down the road. All her bravery had evaporated, all she could think of was getting caught and being sent to a reformatory or a prison! Feeling sick and shaky, she finally reached the Staveley's house. She felt in her pocket. It was empty. Lily had taken the front door key with her – to 1898! Rose sat on the front steps and wept.

It had all been too much: the race to the wool shop, creeping round the house, the cat, Lily disappearing – and now what on earth was she going to say to Sylvia?

She was so busy sobbing she didn't hear the front door open, or notice Sylvia standing behind her, until she felt a comforting arm around her shoulder.

'Rose, darling, whatever is the matter?'

Chapter Thirteen

The Sick Room

Rose looked up at Sylvia with tear-filled eyes. For a moment she thought of telling her everything, right from the beginning. Sylvia was staring up and down the street.

'Where's Lily? Why isn't she with you Rose?'

Rose's stomach clenched and she opened her mouth to try and answer but no words would come out.

Sylvia's expression changed. Now she was the one to sound panicked and tearful. 'Oh my God, he's taken her hasn't he? I knew there was something odd about that note she left. How did he persuade her to go with him? Did you see where they went? Did you try and follow them?'

Rose nodded wordlessly. That way she didn't need to lie out loud and it meant she didn't have to make a story up.

Sylvia clutched at Rose's sleeve. 'Where did they go Rose, have you any idea?'

Rose gulped.

She was going to have to say something or Sylvia might go to the police, and then she really would be in trouble. 'Lily told me she'd agreed to go with her Dad, just for a few days. She just really wanted to see him. She wanted to tell him how happy she is here with you. She hadn't wanted to tell you in case you didn't let her. I didn't see where they went. They drove off really fast in a car. I couldn't see much 'cos it was still dark, but it was Mark, I recognised him from the photo. Lily didn't want you to call the police. She wasn't frightened or anything. She was sure he wouldn't force her to go to America. She said if her dad tried to make her, she'd do a karate chop or something, and run away.'

Sylvia gave a weak smile. 'Yes, I bet she would. Oh dear, I'm so worried! It's typical of Mark to do something silly like this. But perhaps Lily's right – he'd never want to make her unhappy and this'll give her a chance to persuade him leave us alone. I really should report him, but if I do it'll only annoy him more and make him more determined to go to court.'

Sylvia put her head in her hands and Rose had a horrible feeling she might cry. Rose hated it when adults cried – it always sounded so awful, and so serious. But Sylvia raised her head and looked long and hard at Rose. 'So you're *sure* she wanted to go? And you're *sure* she promised to be back in a few days?'

Rose nodded. It wasn't quite a lie – it was just that Lily had travelled in time, not with her dad.

Sylvia frowned. 'I'll give them a few days. If I still haven't heard from Mark then I will have to inform the police. Come on in, Rose. Let's get some breakfast.'

Rose followed her slowly into the house. She didn't feel hungry at all and the cereal clogged up her mouth like sawdust. She hated to see Sylvia so upset and she felt dreadful lying to her. But when she thought of Aubrey, lying sick and gasping on his bed, she knew she'd done the right thing.

Sylvia had decided that Rose should carry on as normal, so after breakfast Rose packed her school bag and set off for St Phillip and St James. It felt odd and lonely walking in by herself. Lily was always such a chatterbox, at least until the school gates. Then she would start to scowl and drag her feet. But Rose had bigger things to worry about than walking in alone. Where *was* Aubrey? And how could she find him as soon as possible? She felt sure he was somewhere in Redland. But without knocking on every door – which would be impossible, there were far too many – how could she tell where he was? Maybe Mrs F could help? But when she thought of the dark, shut-up shop she'd seen that morning she just knew the old lady had gone. What was it Mrs F had said to her? Don't ask so many questions. Trust your instincts. Rose sighed, just at the moment she had no idea what her instincts were.

'Rosie, Rosie, wait for *me*!' It was Ellie from next door. Rosie looked round to see the six year-old racing along, dressed from head to toe in pink. Rose had noticed children nowadays could tell their parents exactly what they wanted to wear. It made her feel quite envious when she thought of all the stiff uncomfortable clothes her mother had forced her into. Ellie's brother, Freddy, was following on behind. He didn't like to be seen walking in with girls, although he'd play quite happily with Rose and Lily in his back garden at home. Today was different, however, as he was bursting to tell someone his news, even a girl.

'Have you heard, Rose…'

'Call her Rosie, like me!' Ellie interrupted.

'Shut up, Smellie!' Freddy elbowed his sister out of the way. 'I'm trying to tell her something. When Mum was buying a paper at the store this morning, that teenager girl – you know the one that's always snogging her boyfriend at the back of the shop – she told Mum there'd been two burglaries: one in Cossins Place and one at the wool shop. The people in Cossins Place were woken by their cat and found their door unlocked, which was really weird 'cos they were sure they'd locked it. And then some people in the church flats heard the alarm go off at the wool shop and when they looked out they saw someone running really fast, into *our* road!'

Rose felt sick with fear but tried hard to make her voice sound normal. 'Did they say what the person looked like?'

'Oh, it was some really rough-looking man, probably escaped from prison or something.'

Rose couldn't help smiling to herself. They obviously hadn't got a good look at her.

Freddy was scowling down at his watch. He was a bit annoyed he hadn't scared Rose more. 'We've still got five minutes before the bell. Lets get some sweets from the corner shop.'

Rose hesitated. Sylvia didn't like them to take sweets into school, but she was feeling so tired and wobbly, and she'd been up since five o'clock. Surely it'd be okay today.

The milky chocolate got her through morning lessons, but by lunch time her head was buzzing with tiredness and it got harder and harder to keep her eyes open. The din of the dining hall gave her a banging headache. Perhaps if I just rest my head on the table for a few seconds, I'll feel better, she thought. The next thing she knew, a large hand with bright red finger nails was shaking her arm.

'Rose – you alright my luvver?' One of the normally very scary dinner ladies was looking down, quite kindly, at her. 'Falling asleep in your pudding? Let's get you to the sick room shall we?'

Before she knew it, Rose was lying in the sick room while Miss Wright went off to ring Sylvia. She came back looking worried. 'No answer. Do you know where she might be?'

Rose remembered Sylvia had a craft fair to get to.

Miss Wright looked back at her list. 'I've got another contact number… looks like it's your neighbour, Fiona Steele. Is that alright?'

Rose nodded. She liked Freddy's mum. She wore masses of black eye make up and always had her hair spiked up like a startled hedgehog. Her husband was Dr Steele, 'the health nut' Rose had seen half-naked on her first morning. He cycled everywhere, usually dressed in brightly coloured, tight-fitting outfits which, topped off by his shiny cycle helmet, made him look like an exotic beetle. The two of them were not at all the kind of parent Rose was used to.

She yawned, trying not to breathe in the smell of stale sick and disinfectant, and stared at the posters on the walls while she waited for Fiona to pick her up. They showed alarming accidents that could happen if you didn't look 'Right, Left and Right again'. There were also pictures of giant nits attacking your hair, and shocking-looking 'germs' that appeared to be killing young children who didn't wash their hands after using the lavatory. Perhaps the 21st century isn't so safe after all, thought Rose with a shiver. At that moment, Fiona rushed in.

'Rose, sweetheart, you poor thing. Lets get you home. You can have a nice lie down in Ellie's room till Sylvia gets back.'

Rose had a pleasant afternoon, being pampered by Fiona with biscuits and hot chocolate. Adults were *so* nice here. They always tried to be kind, and when you spoke they listened as if they really cared about what you were saying. She fell into a deep and dreamless sleep.

A sharp slam of the front door woke her up. It was followed by Richard Steele's cheerful bellow. 'Fo, I'm home!'

'Good day, Rich? Busy?' Rose could hear Fiona walking into the hallway.

'Well, something quite odd happened actually. Damn, my brake lever's slipped. Can you come and hold my bike, Fo? I'll tell you what happened while I fix it. Right, just got to tighten this up... aarrgh!'

'Come on, Rich, the kids'll be home soon. What happened?'

'Yeah, well the police brought this child into casualty. About eleven years-old. He'd been found lying in Cotham Park early this morning by that tree with the milestone in it. Really unwell, unable to talk and no-one with him. Nobody's reported a child missing. It's a complete mystery.'

'What's wrong with him? Why can't he talk? Rich, how long are you going to be? This bike's getting really heavy!'

Rose was on tenterhooks by now and hanging over the banisters trying to catch every word of Dr Steele's story.

'He could hardly breathe, let alone speak. We're not sure what he's got, but we've had to put him on a ventilator – he's really poorly. If only we had a bit more information we could get him started on the right treatment, but at the moment we're really in the dark about what's wrong with him. Good grief, who's that?'

Rose was standing at the top of the stairs looking as white as a sheet. There was no time to worry about the consequences, she had to speak now – however odd it made her look.

'He's got diphtheria – please try to cure him now!'

Both Richard and Fiona stared up at Rose in astonishment.

'Rose, sweetheart, we must have woken you up. Were you having a bad dream?'

'No, I'm fine, thank you. But I do mean it about the diphtheria. I… I saw people with it in Peru and it's just like you described. I'm sure that's what Aub – I mean that boy – has got.'

Dr Steele was staring vaguely into space. 'Hmm, that's very interesting, Rose. It would fit a lot of his symptoms. Of course we wouldn't think about it normally in the UK, because nearly everyone gets immunised – that's an injection that stops you getting it. But you never know, he might have slipped through the net. He could have been travelling abroad and caught it. Its still around in some countries. It would be quite unusual though!'

'Please, Dr Steele, please try and do something. Is there an injection or some tablets you can give him?'

Richard looked at her quizzically. 'You seem very sure he's got it. Do you know something about him?'

'No, no! I… er… knew someone who died of it in Peru and it was just so horrible…' Rose started crying, thinking of poor little Eustace.

Fiona ran up and put her arms around her. 'Oh Rosie, that must have been awful. I'm sure Rich'll get onto it, won't you, Rich?'

Dr Steele nodded. 'I'll ring my junior doctor now. I'll get her to look down his throat. If its diphtheria she should see patches that look like old grey leather. Doctors used to see them and shudder. They knew it meant almost certain death.'

'Rich! You're scaring the poor girl even more!'

Richard looked apologetic. 'Sorry, Rose, didn't mean to upset you. I was just musing to myself. If it is diphtheria we've got an anti-toxin we can give him straight away. He'll have a very good chance of a complete cure.'

There was a loud knocking on the door and Sylvia, looking even more frazzled than usual, burst in. 'Rose, darling, I'm so sorry I wasn't there when the school called. Thank you so much, Fiona for bringing her home. What a day I've had! Did Rose tell you? Lily's spending a few days with her dad – *not* planned – typical Mark! I could really do with a cuppa, thank you, Fiona.'

Fiona was waving a teabag at her and the two of them disappeared into the kitchen. Rose followed. She felt weary but triumphant. She'd followed her instincts. She'd spoken out. And now it looked as if everything might turn out alright after all.

CHAPTER FOURTEEN

Ward 17

That night Rose lay awake in a very quiet and empty-feeling bedroom. She'd got used to Lily's night-time chatter and even missed her snoring. She couldn't help wondering how Lily was getting on – had she found herself under the milestone tree like Aubrey? Was she wandering around the streets of Redland, desperately searching for someone to take her in? She thought for the first time how brave Lily had been. When Rose had wished to escape she had no idea anything would really happen, but when Lily wished, she knew. She knew she'd go back in time – to strange people, living in a strange time. And there was no absolute guarantee of return. They were both putting all their trust in one old woman and her mysterious wool shop. Suppose Aubrey did die? Suppose Dr Steele couldn't really save him? That would leave one person here in this time and two in the past. Then who would swap with who? And who would get left behind?

Rose shivered and pulled the covers up over her head.

'Aubrey will get better. He *will*!' She repeated it over and over in her mind, willing it to be true, and at some point – she couldn't tell when – she fell off to sleep.

The next morning, in the middle of a rather subdued breakfast, there was a loud rap at the door. Richard Steele, looking like a bumblebee in his black and yellow cycling outfit and helmet, was standing, grinning on the doorstep. 'Congratulations, Rose! That was an absolutely inspired guess of yours. We checked the boy's throat again and there it was… the classic wash leather appearance. You were quite right! It was diphtheria. We whacked in the anti-toxin and started him on some antibiotics and he's already a different child. Still not saying much and seems a bit confused, but well on the way to recovery – thanks to you, Rose!'

Rose felt a huge wave of relief. She'd done it. She'd helped save Aubrey's life! 'Can I see him please, Dr Steele?'

Richard looked surprised. 'Erm, well children aren't normally allowed on the ward, unless they're family.' He looked down at Rose's pleading dark eyes. 'But I suppose, as he doesn't appear to have any family, we could make an exception. And after all you may well have saved his life, so it seems like a fair cop. He's still fairly fragile though, so just a quick visit.'

'Thank you! Thank you!' Rose was hopping up and down with excitement.

'Her mother's been very ill, you see,' put in Sylvia, as though that explained Rose's odd behaviour.

'Well, okay,' smiled Richard. He turned and started to push his bike down the steps. 'Visiting's 4 – 6.30pm. He's on Ward 17. Bye now.'

Rose couldn't wait for the school day to end. Sylvia had agreed to pick her up at the school gates and walk with her up to the

Children's Hospital. Rose was beside herself with excitement at the thought of seeing Aubrey. It would prove that this was all really happening, that she wasn't some sort of ghost and that she really had saved his life. There was also a part of her that was just looking forward to seeing *him*. She'd missed his cheeky smile and the way he always came up and chatted to her – even though she was often quite rude back. He was different from other boys. If only her mother had let her, they might even have been friends.

Rose followed Sylvia up St Michael's Hill. It was so steep at the top you felt as though you were teetering on the edge of a cliff and might topple off into the city below. Bristol was set out in a wide bowl beneath them. It was the first time that Rose had seen it in the 21st century and it made her gasp. Everything was pinpoint clear. There were no clouds of black smoke from factory chimneys, in fact not a single wisp escaped from the higgledy-piggledy chimney pots below her. She could see right across the harbour and way over to Dundry hill beyond. It was amazing. A steady throb of noise came up from the roads which were packed nose to tail with motor cars. Rose jumped in terror as a white vehicle screamed by them, a blue light flashing from its roof.

Sylvia patted her arm reassuringly. 'It's just an ambulance, sweetie. I don't suppose you saw many of them out in your village. Here we are!' She stopped in front of a large pink-stoned building with ' Bristol Children's Hospital' engraved above an imposing porch way. 'Now let me see…' Sylvia consulted a crumpled bit of paper with Richard's scrawled, handwriting on it. 'Ward 17, third floor, first door on the right as you get out of the lift.' Sylvia pushed her woolly hat back from her forehead – it was purple and covered in large bobbles – and marched up the steps.

They were soon lost in a maze of identical corridors and Sylvia was looking flustered. 'I do hate hospitals, Rose. They always have such a bad aura.' Sylvia had worn a crystal necklace for the visit. 'To neutralise the negative vibrations, Rose darling.' She had tried to persuade Rose to wear one too, but in Rose's experience crystals were not a force to be meddled with so she'd politely said no. Now, staring down the endless grey corridors, she wondered if she could have done with a bit of crystal magic.

Rose had never been in a hospital before. She'd had chicken pox and measles and mumps, but they'd all been treated by Dr Ormorod at home. Even when Father had been so ill, they'd never thought of taking him to hospital. Hospitals were for poor people, or if you had something really infectious like scarlet fever, or diphtheria.

'The lift!' Rose rushed forward and pointed at a small sign stuck high on the wall that they'd previously missed. 'Come on. It's just around the corner.'

Rose was excited at the thought of travelling in a lift. She'd seen pictures of them in her *Sunday Annual*, but she'd never actually been in one. Sylvia pressed a glowing red button and two metal doors glided apart, revealing a small boxy room that they stepped into, the doors shutting with a firm whoosh behind them.

'Do you want to press the button – or are you too old for all that?'

Rose looked at the array of buttons on the panel in front of her and shook her head. She hadn't a clue which one to press. Sylvia leaned over and pushed number three. There was a grinding judder and then a sudden whoosh upwards. Rose, taken by surprise, staggered and fell against the side of the lift.

'Rose, darling – everything alright?' Sylvia looked concerned.

Rose nodded weakly trying to look as though she wasn't hanging onto the walls. Then as suddenly as they'd started they stopped and the doors slid open. Rose dashed out, giving the departing lift a terrified stare.

'Is it okay if we take the stairs on the way out?' she gulped.

'Yes of course. It's terribly claustrophobic in those things isn't it?' Sylvia was looking at her piece of paper again. 'Here it is, ward 17. We've just made it in time for visiting hours.'

They passed through a set of swing doors and into a long ward full of rather well-looking children, most of them sitting up and chatting cheerfully to their families. There was no sign of Aubrey.

Sylvia marched down to a cluster of nurses and after a short discussion beckoned Rose towards a side room. The door to the room was closed and the small window in the top of the door was covered by a blind. Rose felt her heart lurch. Suppose it wasn't Aubrey, suppose they opened the door and found a different boy, a strange boy, lying ill in the bed?

'Come on, Rose. Sister said we should only stay a few minutes because he's very weak still.' Sylvia disappeared through the door.

Rose could hear a low murmuring as Sylvia started talking to whoever was inside. She took a deep breath and pushed open the door.

It was Aubrey. He was lying in a large metal bed and wearing a blue gown with animals all over it – Rose guessed he must have been given this by the hospital. His face, always pale, was now as white as the pillow he lay on, which made his freckles even more notice-able as they spilled out over his nose and cheeks. His hair looked longer and darker than she remembered it, and was pushed back damply from his forehead. He was looking in a slightly puzzled way at Sylvia – who hadn't taken her hat off and so was looking rather odd. He didn't notice Rose immediately. Maybe he thought she was just another nurse come to take his temperature. It made her want to shout at him: 'It's me, Rose Cox, I'm really here!' But she knew she mustn't.

Sylvia was chatting away. 'You're doing awfully well. I'm sure you'll be feeling much better soon. Look, I've brought a visitor for you – you don't know each other, but it's just nice to have someone your own age to talk to, isn't it?'

With some effort Aubrey turned his head towards Rose. He stared at her. His eyes were completely blank. Rose's heart sank. He doesn't recognise me! Why doesn't he recognise me? Then, like a light being switched on, recognition washed across Aubrey's face and his mouth creased up into his familiar grin. Hurriedly Rose put her fingers up to her lips and tried to signal, with lots of wiggling of eyebrows, that he mustn't show he knew her. Then she started to speak. 'I expect you're awfully tired and can't say much. I bet your throat is really sore and everything. You're probably feeling a bit peculiar and confused – I know what that's like…' Rose glanced nervously over at Sylvia. It was so difficult to say everything she wanted to say without giving herself away. 'I've travelled a long way from home too, so I know how strange every-thing must feel. I'm sure everything is going to be alright though, and you'll get back home to your family as soon as possible. I'm going to come back when you're feeling a bit better and we can have a really long talk then – just the two of us.'

Sylvia looked surprised. 'Well, that's very kind of you, Rose. We'll have to check with the staff if that would be alright.' She turned back to Aubrey. 'I think we better leave you now. The nurses said just a few minutes. Goodbye, and take care.' She patted his head affectionately and walked out into the corridor.

Quickly, Rose dashed to the side of the bed. 'I *will* be back. Then I'll explain everything to you, I promise.'

Aubrey's face suddenly crumpled and he looked very small and lost. Without thinking Rose leaned over and planted a kiss on his soft black hair. She heard a creak as the door opened again and a nurse bustled into the room. Rose leapt back blushing, then, turning to give a last wave, she let herself out of the room.

'Goodbye, Aubrey,' she mouthed and was pleased to see his face relax into a smile as he waved weakly back.

Rose felt a bit flat as she walked home. It had been so exciting to see Aubrey, but so short, and then having to leave him all alone in that hospital room. And she was going back to a house with no Lily in it. No-one to chat to or share secrets with. Rose began to feel seriously sorry for herself. Then she remembered something Lily had said, just as she was disappearing. 'I'll try and contact you. Look under the milestone tree'.

'Sylvia, would it be alright if I went to the park when we get back? I feel like a breath of fresh air.'

'Okay, darling – but see if Freddy and Ellie want to go too. I'd prefer you not to go by yourself.'

'I'll be alright honestly. I know the way, I've been there loads of times – I mean with Lily of course.' Rose blushed. She still had to be very careful what she said to grown-ups, particularly now Lily wasn't around to cover up for her.

'No, sweetie. I don't like the thought of you going alone. Just call round to the Steele's' and ask them if they'll go with you.'

Rose groaned inwardly. Honestly, parents nowadays were almost as bad as Victorian ones sometimes. There was no way around it, so once they were back on Brighton Road Rose went next door and knocked reluctantly at Freddy's door. Didn't grown-ups know how embarrassing it was for a girl to ask a boy her age to go to the park with her? She hoped Ellie would be there – that would make it slightly easier. But when Fiona answered the door she told Rose that Ellie was at a party.

'But Fred's here. Freddy!' she yelled up the stairs as Rose stood, mortified, on the step. 'Rose wants to know if you'll go to the park with her.'

'Err, what for? I mean why?' Freddy yelled back.

'Fred, that's not very polite. Come down here and talk properly to us.'

'I'm in the middle of a game. If I stop now I'll lose all my points and I won't make the next level!'

Fiona looked exasperated. 'Leave that wretched computer game for a minute and come and have a normal conversation – now!'

Rose was wishing the ground would swallow her up as Freddy came down the stairs, kicking furiously at each banister on the way.

'Right, young man, it's some fresh air for you. Staring at a screen and playing those violent games is no way to spend a lovely day like today.'

Groaning, Freddy stuffed his feet into a pair of trainers.

'*Not* like that. Undo the laces first!' Fiona raised her eyebrows and sighed dramatically at Rose. 'Boys, eh Rose? I don't suppose you give Sylvia this sort of trouble?'

It was true, but Rose was pretty sure this was not the time to say so. After all she was going to have to spend the next hour or so with this particular boy, whether she liked it or not.

Freddy banged out of the house and set off up the road, shoulders hunched, sending thunderous glances back at Rose as she hurried after him. She couldn't help thinking how different it would have been walking with Aubrey. He would have hung back to chat with her. He might even have brought his skates and taught her to use them, just as he'd promised he would. But it was no use wishing; she was stuck with Freddy. She just had to think of a way of distracting him once they got to the park, so she could look for that message under the milestone tree.

When they arrived at the iron gates, the park was full of school children tearing around with their shirts untucked. Their bags and coats had been thrown down in heaps on the grass. There were clusters of mothers surrounded by pushchairs and screeching toddlers, and a group of older boys were kicking a football on a piece of tarmac in front of the swings.

'Mind if I join them?' asked Freddy. But he was already heading off, pulling his sweatshirt over his head. Rose breathed a sigh of relief. She walked slowly up the winding path towards the top of the park. She had spotted the milestone tree the first time she'd come to the park with Lily. It was so enormous she could hardly believe it was the same tiny sapling that she'd seen planted in her own time. Rose knelt under the huge green canopy of leaves. The gritty earth pressed painfully into her knees as she leaned forwards to run her hands over the metal milestone. There was a long crack that ran from the top, with its carving of a Tudor Rose, to its base – now embedded deep in the roots of the tree. It was so completely buried in the bark she could hardly make out the edges, and the embossed lettering was worn and almost lost under moss and lichen. She remembered it shiny and new, although she couldn't quite remember the exact words written on it. All she could read now were: Planted…Alderman…Commemorated…2 Miles… Majesty.

Rose sighed as she looked around the base of the tree. There were no clues here as to where Lily might have left a message. Suppose the tree had grown so much it was now *underneath* the tree? But no. Lily would have thought of that. She knew what the tree looked like in modern times. So, if she was Lily, where would she think of hiding a message so it could still be found over a hundred years later?

Rose closed her eyes and scrunched her nails into the palms of her hands; the shrieks and yells from the park faded away till all she could hear was the whispering of the leaves gently swaying above her. She opened her eyes and found herself staring, very hard, at blade of grass a few feet in front of the milestone. There, she thought, that's where it will be!

She had managed to slip a small trowel of Sylvia's into her pocket and, after a quick check that no-one was watching, she began to dig. It was hard work. The ground was stony and knobbly with roots. She had to stop every time someone passed by, in case they reported her for damaging park property. Gradually the hole deepened.

If I don't find it soon I'll have to stop and come back after dark, Rose thought miserably. Someone is bound to notice what I'm doing soon. She shoved the trowel in for one last try and then, quite distinctly, she heard a clink. Probably just a stone, she told herself, not wanting to get too excited. Carefully she scraped away the damp soil. No, it wasn't a stone, it was a small and very rusty metal box. Rose started scraping furiously around its edges until she could jam the tip of her trowel underneath to start levering it up.

'What on earth are you doing?'

Rose snapped round. Freddy was standing over her, one arm curled around his football, the other pushing back his hair from his sweaty forehead.

'I came to fetch the ball,' he added as though he owed Rose an explanation for spying on her.

'I… um… like digging things up from the past. You know, coins and stuff. It's just an old box. Someone must have buried it ages ago and forgotten about it.'

Rose desperately wanted Freddy to go away, so she could open the box and see if there was a message from Lily in it. But Freddy turned and kicked the ball back down to his friends, then squatted down besides her. Before she could stop him he'd reached into the hole and yanked the box out. It was covered in soil and the metal catch on one side was clogged with earth. Freddy banged it sharply against the milestone and the top flew open.

'Please give it to me,' Rose begged. 'It's really important. And anyway I was the one who found it!'

She tried to grab it back, but Freddy was too quick for her. He whipped it behind his back. He didn't like being told what to do, particularly by a girl.

'Why's it so important? I don't believe you found it by accident. You knew it was there, didn't you?'

Rose thought fast. She was going to have to do something, but what could she say that would make him give it back? She couldn't tell him about the time travel. There was only one thing for it.

'*Whaa! Oah, wha-ooh!*' Rose buried her face in her arms and did her best fake crying.

It had an immediate effect.

'Oh, for God's sake stop it! Here's your stupid box. There's nothing in it any way – look!'

Freddy held the tin upside down, shook it several times, then threw it onto the grass. Then he stomped off back down to his mates and his girl-free game of football.

For a few moments Rose sat staring at the empty box, a huge well of disappointment building up inside her. She had so wanted there to be a message from Lily. She missed her and she really, really hoped she was alright. And there wouldn't to be any other way of finding out. Sadly, she turned the rusty tin over in her hands; there was nothing in it just cold metal sides. She slipped her fingers down inside. The bottom wasn't metal: it felt like cardboard or...

Yes! It was thick paper, jammed into the base of the box. She tried to prise it out with her fingernails and a little piece crumbled away – she was going to have to do this very carefully. Little by little she manoeuvred it up the sides of the tin, until at last it was free in her hand: a yellow sheet of paper, very dry and crackly, one side jagged as though it had been torn quickly out of a book. There was faint blue writing on it, scrawled, as though written in a hurry. Some of the letters were smudged with damp and mildew so Rose had to bring it right up to her face to read.

The note was in Lily's handwriting and it was shockingly brief:

> *HELP! You must get me back NOW!!*
> *'L'*

The letter was dated the 17th of June. Rose checked the date on her watch – that was tomorrow!

Chapter Fifteen

The Axted's Establishment For Young Ladies

Lily lay still, her eyes closed, but all her other senses acutely alert. Around her she could feel a stiff cotton material – maybe sheets? Above her was an unaccustomed weight. Blankets? Or an eiderdown? She was wearing something very long which was rather tight around her neck and wrists; she guessed it was a nightdress. When she sniffed there was a musty smell, like coal dust and shoe polish and sweat all mixed up together. Outside she could hear birds chirruping and trilling, far louder than she was used to at home. Home! Lily's heart lurched. She definitely wasn't at home, but where on earth was she?

She remembered sitting on the iron bedstead with Rose watching her and she remembered holding the piece of crystal. Lily checked. Yes she was still holding it, she could feel the sharp edges pressing into the palm of her hand. But after that it was all a blank, how much time had passed since then? She should really open her eyes and check her watch. She felt for her wrist – it was bare, her watch had vanished!

I've got to do it. I've got to open my eyes. Lily felt a wave of panic at the thought. If she opened them, and she wasn't at home in her own bed, it would mean she'd really done it, really travelled in time, and that would be the most terrifying thing that had ever happened to her. She forced her eyelids to open. The room she was in was quite light. The bed was under a window, hung with tattered blue and white striped curtains. The walls were covered in a cream wallpaper embossed with daffodils that matched the eiderdown on her bed.

She turned her head and looked over to the other side of the room, then quickly snapped her eyes shut again. Against the far wall was a double bed and in that bed were two shapes – and the head of one of those shapes was staring straight at Lily.

Lily lay still, her heart hammering against her chest. There was silence. Then she heard the double bed creaking and light footsteps pattering across the floor. She knew someone was standing by her bed; she could hear them breathing.

Lily was so frightened she thought she might be sick. The breathing came closer. It was right by her ear now. Just when Lily thought she could bear it no longer the shape spoke. 'I saw you.'

The voice sounded young, probably a girl, around six or seven.

'I saw you looking at me. I know you're awake.'

Slowly Lily opened her eyes. Standing in front of her was a small child with long fair hair, dressed in a white night dress that covered her feet. There was elaborate lace stitching on the front of it, but it was worn and patched at the elbows. She was staring inquisitively at Lily with large blue eyes.

'Did you come in that carriage last night? I heard the horses outside.'

Lily wondered what to do. What had Rose done on her first

day? Oh yes – she'd kept quiet and nodded a lot. Lily nervously jerked her chin up and down.

The girl seemed satisfied with this, but carried on with her questions. 'Was it right in the middle of the night? I never heard you come up to bed.'

'Of course you didn't, silly. You were too busy snoring in my ear.' On the other side of the room a larger girl had sat up in bed and was sleepily rubbing her eyes. 'Annie must have let you in after we all went to bed. Was your coach delayed?'

Lily gave another nod. The older girl frowned at her. 'We thought you weren't coming till next week. Did your father change his plans?'

The older girl also had fair hair, but a longer, more serious face than the younger one. Lily decided they must be sisters. She also decided she would have to try speaking now. 'Yes, he did. It was all, um, very last minute...' She tailed off, afraid of giving herself away. Perhaps if she tried a question herself it would stop them asking *her* so many. 'Who's Annie?'

'She's the youngest of the Miss Axteds. There are three of them. Mary, Dora and Annie. You have to call Mary and Dora "Miss", but Annie's just "Annie".' The small girl leaned in confidingly. 'They treat her a bit like a maid because they don't think she's as clever as them. But actually she's by far the nicest. Miss Mary is a real horror!'

'*Edie*! It's not Christian to talk about them like that.' Her elder sister frowned furiously at her but the little girl ignored her and carried on.

'There's an older brother. Reginald. He's in India, in the Army.

They go on and on about how wonderful he is and we have to include him in Sunday prayers, but if you look at his photo you can see he looks just like a tomato. Doesn't he, Frances?'

'*Edie*!' Frances was looking despairing. 'You *must* behave! You know how Miss Mary likes to listen in at doors. If she heard you say anything against Reginald you'd be on bread and water for a week.'

At that precise moment the door swung open. 'Edith! What are you doing out of bed? You know it's forbidden before six o'clock.'

A very tall, severe-looking woman stood in the doorway. She was dressed in a long grey skirt and a striped blouse buttoned right up to her chin. Her hair was stretched back from her face in a tightly coiled bun. She stared disapprovingly around the room and when her gaze fell on Lily, who was cowering under her bed covers, a look of shock and then fury crossed her face.

'Ye Gods and little fishes! *Who* let this child in here?' She turned back to glare at Edie and Frances, whose fault she obviously thought this was.

Edie looked delighted. She had never, in all her time at the Axted's School for Young Ladies, heard the sisters utter anything stronger than 'Oh Dear'. 'Ye Gods and little fishes' – she would remember that one!

Frances realised she was going to have to save the situation before Miss Mary got even angrier. 'Please Miss Mary, it's the new girl – the one we were expecting next week. Her father changed his plans. Annie must have let her in late last night.'

Miss Axted looked at Lily, fury now turning into annoyance. 'Well, how very inconvenient! I presume your father sent a telegram explaining the alteration? I shall have to have a word with that telegraph boy. This isn't the first time we've had trouble with the post. Really, one wonders what one is paying for sometimes. You will find we are not prepared for you at all. In fact my sister Annie left on the early train to Bath to look after an elderly aunt. We didn't think we would be needing her until next week. So we shall be rather short staffed.'

Lily breathed a secret sigh of relief. If Annie wasn't back until next week it meant there was nobody to challenge her story of arriving in the night. That meant she'd made it through the first hurdle in her new world.

Miss Axted was striding over to the window where she wrenched back the curtains, her face still lined with indignation. 'Well, at least your trunk was sent on ahead, so you will have all your clothes. Although Annie has not had the time to unpack it because – as you know – we were not expecting you so soon.' Miss Axted paused and looked round at the three of them. 'This has been a very unusual and trying start to the day, girls, but now we must carry on with our normal routine. Get yourselves washed, dressed and downstairs for morning prayers in fifteen minutes. And no shilly-shallying, Edith. I won't put up with any tardiness this morning. I already have *quite* enough to deal with.'

With that last instruction she swept out of the room, leaving Lily to climb out of bed and look nervously at the large leather-bound trunk in front of her. Embossed in gold letters on the front were the letters: *L. J. L. D.*

For the first time Lily could also see what she was wearing. As she'd suspected, it was a thick cotton nightdress. The buttons were small, flat and very fiddly, so she decided to yank it off over her head. Immediately there were squeaks and gasps from across the room.

'What are you *doing*?' hissed Frances. 'We always dress *under* our night clothes. Suppose someone were to walk in?'

Embarrassed, Lily walked over to the trunk. She pulled open the heavy lid and a sheet of tissue paper wafted out across the floor. Inside were neatly folded garments, each one packed between layers of tissue. But which ones should she wear? Lily tried desperately to recall the lesson she'd had on Victorian clothes, but all she could remember was that there was a lot of complicated underwear. She glanced over at the other girls, hoping for some clues, but they'd been too fast for her and were already pulling on dresses and pinafores.

Lily thought hard for a few moments and then turned to the sisters. 'Oh dear! I don't think my maid has packed my smalls.' It was something she'd heard her granny say to describe her knickers, so she hoped it would be polite enough for Victorian times.

Frances came over and peered into the box. 'Yes, she did. They're underneath the pinafores.' She picked out some long bloomers and a strange vest with ribbons and buttons hanging from it, followed by a stiff underskirt and a pair of long black stockings.

'Come on, Lily. The Axeheads will be pouring steam out of their ears if we're late again.' Edie was bouncing up and down by the bedroom door.

'Don't call them that, Edie. One of these days they'll hear you and then you'll be in fearful trouble.' Frances was plaiting her hair and tying perfect, symmetrical bows on each side.

Lily, meanwhile, was struggling into the underwear. She couldn't work out how the stocking attached to the ribbons so she just folded over the tops and hoped for the best. She selected a navy blue dress that wasn't too showy – she had a feeling the Axteds wouldn't approve of some of the more elaborate ones in the trunk – and then finished off with a white pinafore like the other girls.

'Ready!'

Frances looked her over critically. 'You must brush your hair and tie it back. I'll lend you one of my ribbons if you like. Oh, and make sure you have your handkerchief – they always check.'

'Time to go!' Edie was still hopping up and down. Lily glanced over at the large clock on the mantelpiece. The elaborate hands pointed to exactly 6.15am. Good heavens, thought Lily, if I were at home I wouldn't even be awake now. Then another thought struck her, something that had been niggling at the back of her mind since Edie had told her to hurry up. Edie had known her name. She'd called her 'Lily'.

Edie and Frances led the way down a curved staircase. A strip of worn carpet ran down the centre of the chipped wooden steps.

'You mustn't run your hand down the banister, because the Miss Axteds say it leaves a dirty mark. They like you to walk like this…' Frances clasped her hands demurely behind her back as she descended into the hallway.

It was so gloomy in the hall that it took a few seconds for Lily's eyes to adjust and take in her surroundings. In contrast to their bare bedroom, it was stuffed with large pieces of dark furniture. The remaining wall space was filled with sepia-tinted photographs and gold-framed pictures of brooding landscapes. Lily shivered. What had she let herself in for?

162

Morning prayers were held in the dining room and the girls stood around a large table, draped with a heavy damask cloth. Edie and Frances immediately dropped their eyes and folded their hands over their aprons, but Lily couldn't help peeping up as the door opened and three very tall women marched in. One she recognised at once as Miss Mary, another was obviously her younger sister. That must be Dora, thought Lily. The third was dressed entirely in black with a curious half veil over her face. Even so, Lily could see she was considerably older than the other two. That must be their mother, she guessed. The original Mrs Axted. The three women stood at the head of the table in front of a huge, grey marble fireplace. They towered over the little girls, their faces set and severe.

The older woman turned and stared grimly at Lily, for what felt like hours, before finally clearing her throat and speaking in a hoarse, dry voice. 'So this is the new girl who arrived so inconsiderately in the middle of the night?'

Lily gulped. Was she meant to reply? Probably not, judging by Mrs Axted's expression. Her terrifying eyes raked over Lily's appearance from head to toe.

'And is it the fashion in Leeds to leave off your shoes like a street urchin?'

Lily heard Frances and Edie gasp as they looked down at her stocking feet. Lily started to tremble and, as her bottom lip began to wobble, she realised she was very close to tears. But I mustn't cry. I mustn't break down. I must be brave! Lily told herself. She put her hands behind her back and pinched her arm hard. It was a trick she'd learnt at school when she was being teased in the

163

playground. The sudden pain took her mind off the awful Mrs Axted and the trembling calmed down.

'I'm sorry, miss, I mean m'am...'

The younger daughter suddenly spoke up. 'Mama, I believe Lily had a very tiring journey yesterday and perhaps is not feeling quite herself. I'll take her upstairs after breakfast and find her some suitable footwear.'

Lily smiled thankfully at her. She could see there was a real kindness behind Miss Dora's strict exterior and she was very grateful for it.

Morning prayers seemed to go on forever. Mrs Axted led them and she had a lot to pray about. She asked the Lord to make them virtuous, humble, respectful and, most importantly, free from sin in all its forms. She then went on to list these in detail and at length. Lily's mind began to drift off to more pressing matters. How long was she going to be here? How was she going to get back? She'd hidden the crystal under the mattress, but how would she know when to use it?

She was brought back down to earth by a sudden rise in Mrs Axted's voice which seemed to be aimed directly at her.

'So where would you rather be – in a beautiful sunny garden or a dark, underground dungeon?'

Lily was confused. Was this real question? Should she answer it?

She risked opening her eyes – no, all the others still had theirs firmly shut. So it must be part of the prayers.

This was confirmed as the old lady continued. 'But there is far worse a darkness than the gloom of the dungeon, far brighter a radiance than the summer sunshine. Sin is a darker, more horrible and deadly prison than anything mere mortals could devise and the only way to save yourselves is by opening your heart to let in the light of Jesus. Let us sing!'

There was a rustle of silk and a clicking of knees as the family rose to their feet, closely followed by Lily, who was anxious not to draw any more attention to herself. Frances shoved a hymn book at her as they all burst into song. Edie sang like an angel whilst the Axteds warbled and screeched like seagulls.

> *There's a sunshine in my soul today*
> *More glorious and bright*
> *Than dwells in any earthly sky*
> *For Jesus is my light!*

Lily mouthed along with the words as best she could and joined in with the loud Amen at the end. She wished now she'd paid more attention to assemblies at Phil and Jim, instead of daydreaming about what was for lunch. She could tell they were going to expect her to know an awful lot more about God and Sinning than she actually did.

Mrs Axted commanded them back down on their knees. This time she had a long list of people to remember in their prayers: 'In particular our dear brother Reginald, who is serving the Empire in Cosipore. May God keep him safe and help him to resist the temptations of this evil world – especially that of strong drink!'

Edie snorted into her handkerchief and Frances had to give her a sharp jab with her elbow to stop her giggling. Mrs Axted gave the girls a dark look and carried on. 'Lastly let us remember the child Horace, an innocent lamb so recently taken back into the arms of Jesus.'

A cold shiver ran down Lily's spine. Horace was Aubrey's little brother, the one who'd died of diphtheria. When Rose had talked about him she hadn't thought of him as a real boy, he was just someone from history, who'd died a long time ago. But actually, he was a child that Edie, Frances and the Axteds all knew. He was very real to them *and* he was the reason she was here, so she could save Aubrey and stop him dying too!

Chapter Sixteen

The Schoolroom

Finally the last Amen was said and they were allowed to get to their feet. Lily's knees were sore from so much kneeling and she hobbled up the stairs after Miss Dora, remembering not to hang on to the banisters on the way up. Dora went through her trunk and pulled out a pair of soft leather shoes which fastened with a little button.

'These will do dear. But goodness what *has* happened to your stockings?'

Lily's stockings hung in rolls around her ankles and as fast as she yanked them up they fell back down again.

'Not like that dear! Really a girl of your age should be able to fasten their own stockings. Does your maid still dress you?' Lily nodded. it seemed better to look dumb than be caught out pretending to know things she didn't. Dora knelt down and showed her the ribbons hanging from her long vest and how to press the rubber buttons through the metal clasps to secure the tops of the stockings in place. It was very fiddly and Lily was not at all sure she'd be able to do it again tomorrow. Maybe I'll just sleep in them, she thought. No one'll notice under that huge nightie!

Dora stood up, her face taking on the severe expression she'd worn when Lily had first seen her. 'We will expect you to dress yourself from now on. I do hope you are not going to be one of those very spoilt children. My sisters and I will not tolerate that.'

'Oh no, I promise I'll do it all myself. I'm really sorry Do – I mean Miss Dora.'

Dora's face softened again. 'Very well, dear. Let us go down for breakfast.'

Breakfast was served on the large dining table that they had been praying around earlier. A stiff, white table-cloth had been thrown over it and some rather chipped bowls and plates laid out. Lily's stomach was rumbling with hunger, but there didn't seem to be any actual food on the table. A skinny, frightened-looking maid appeared holding a silver tray which she placed in front of Mrs Axted. It was piled with sausages, bacon, eggs and a stack of golden toast dripping butter. The girls watched enviously as the Miss Axteds began tucking into the feast. Meanwhile, the maid reappeared with a tureen filled with thin, grey porridge. She dripped a few spoonfuls of the nasty-looking sludge into each of the girls' bowls. Edie made a gagging noise and Miss Mary stopped chewing her sausage for a moment to fix her with a disapproving stare.

'Edith, stop making that dreadful face. There are people in Africa who would give their eye teeth to have the food in your bowl.' Edie stared at her porridge and muttered quietly. 'Well I would give my eye teeth *not* to have it.'

Unfortunately for Edie, she did not speak quietly enough. A red flush started to make its way up Mary's neck. This, Lily would learn over the next few days, was not a good sign.

'Edith, in the corner, now! I shall keep your porridge and you shall eat it cold at luncheon.'

On their way back up to their room, Frances told Lily that Edie spent most breakfasts in the corner.

'But when Annie's here she usually manages to lose the bowl before lunchtime!' Edie put in cheerfully.

'Dora seems quite nice though,' Lily sat on her bed swinging her legs.

Frances frowned, 'She's alright, but she's not always on our side.'

'And Mary's the worst; she's nearly as bad as her mother. No one will ever marry them you know!' Edie announced gleefully.

'Why?' asked Lily. 'Because they're so horrible?'

'No silly, even horrible people get married – look at Mrs Axted!' Edie collapsed in giggles whilst Frances sighed, exasperated.

'No, it's because they have no money. Mrs Axted's a widow and her husband…' Frances lowered her voice, 'drank!' Lily tried to look suitably horrified as Frances continued. 'So the only way they can stay in the house is to run it as a school, charge our parents lots of money and give us dreadful food. Reginald is supposed to send part of his salary from India but he never does. He spends it all on…'

'Drink!' interrupted Edie again and started rolling around on the bed making glugging noises.

'Shush, Edie,' Frances waved her hand towards the door. 'They'll hear!'

Sure enough, there was the sound of footsteps on the bare

floorboards outside. The door swung open to reveal Miss Mary. Luckily there was no sigh of a red flush on her neck. Edie had got away with it this time. Miss Mary clapped her hands sharply.

'Now girls, get your mending together. I don't suppose you have any yet, Lily, but you can work on some of Edie's. Her stockings always need darning, I really don't know how she makes such terrible holes in them.'

Miss Mary supervised the girls for needlework: she gave Lily a mushroom-shaped object which she had to push inside the toe of the stocking and then weave back and forth until she'd sewn a patch. Lily was very bad at this.

'Couldn't I do some knitting instead? I'm really quite good at that,' she begged. But Mary was unrelenting.

'No you shall do as you're told – this isn't Liberty Hall you know!'

The mending session took place in silence. Lily was beginning to realise what the Victorian's meant when they said children should be seen and not heard. Half-way through she became desperate to go to the loo, but she had no idea how to go about asking for Miss Mary's permission. As soon as they were finished she whispered urgently to Frances, who asked for her. 'Please may I take Lily to wash her hands?'

She led Lily through the kitchen to the lavatory. To her relief, Lily saw it was very much like their one at home, although a bit smellier and it looked in need of a good clean. It had *The Acme Thunderer* inscribed around the bowl – which Lily thought sounded a bit rude. On her way back through the narrow kitchen, she saw the worried-looking maid from breakfast washing some pots in a stone sink by the window. A red-faced woman, who Lily guessed was the cook, was shovelling coal into the bottom of a stove. Neither of them stopped what they were doing or gave Lily a second glance. Its almost as if they can't see me, she thought. Maybe I'm like a ghost here? Maybe they really can't see me? But once out in the hallway Edie came bounding up to her, making her feel quite real and normal again.

'Time for lessons. Are you very swotty? The last girl was and it made me and Frances look like we were complete dunces!'

'I'm not bad,' considered Lily. 'But I think you might have done a lot of subjects that I haven't.'

She was proved horribly right. Miss Dora took the first lesson and it was Maths – never Lily's favourite subject at the best of times.

'Now girls, today we'll be concentrating on 'Compound Interest'. Get your books out please.'

Lily felt a rush of panic. What on earth was 'Compound Interest'? Despite Dora's best efforts to explain it to her, Lily's sums stubbornly refused to add up. Meanwhile Frances, and even little Edie, were earning rows of ticks. Miss Dora examined Lily's page, which was full of scrawled crossings out. She shook her head sadly.

'My dear, I can see your education has been sadly neglected. I'll have to take you all the way back to Book One.'

Edie sniggered and Lily glowered furiously at her. She could see why Frances got fed up with her little sister sometimes. The next lesson, Geography, was no better. Now Lily had thought she would be quite good at this. After all, she'd got an A-star for her rivers project last term. But she had no chance to shine in Miss Dora's lesson. They were each given a map of the world and instructed to colour in pink the countries belonging to the British Empire. Lily chewed the top of her pencil for a long time before trying Spain. Dora shook her head. She tried again. France perhaps? Dora looked shocked. Last go. Lily took a deep breath and went for Russia. Dora ripped the map away from her.

'Really Lily! I do believe you have been sent here to try us.' Miss Dora took a few deep breaths and smoothed down the pleats of her dress. 'Let us hope Greek goes a little better for you.'

It didn't of course, and by the end of the morning both Lily and Miss Dora were completely frazzled. Dora dabbed at her forehead with a lace hanky. 'Dear, dear! Well I think we could all do with a constitutional. Perhaps it will blow some of those cobwebs away, Lily.'

Lily had no idea what her teacher was talking about. What on earth was a constitutional? It turned out to be 'a walk' and there was a huge amount of stiff, outdoor clothing to be pulled on before they could go on it. *I can't believe they wear all this in summer!* thought Lily. She was already too hot under her thick coat, hat and gloves. The boots she was given were far too small and pointy and she could only just squeeze her feet into them. Miss Dora tutted impatiently as Lily tried to pull the eyelets over the buttons to do them up;

'Do you require a button hook child? Really at this rate we shall be here all day!'

'No, no I'm fine. I've just got the last one to do…' Lily yanked it into place and followed the girls out of the large, green front door.

'Carefully down the steps. And no running or shouting Edie!'

Miss Dora turned to Lily. 'Quiet, suitable conversation is allowed – the weather or spiritual matters, for example.'

At last, thought Lily, a chance to talk and get some more information from the other girls. Miss Dora was walking a little way ahead, so hopefully she wouldn't hear if they said anything 'unsuitable'.

'How long have you been here?' she asked Frances, as they made their way down the road. Frances frowned.

'Two years, two months and three days, counting today.'

Lily was taken aback by Frances's exactness. 'So you're counting, like prisoners do in their cells?'

'Shh!' Frances looked nervously at Dora's back. 'Well, obviously it's not as awful as prison, but it's not nearly as nice as being at home.'

'With your mother?'

Frances whole body stiffened. Lily realised too late she'd said the wrong thing.

'Mama is dead. She died three years ago…'

'That's why we're here,' interrupted Edie, who was tired of being left out of the conversation. 'Because Papa married an evil witch and now they have their very own baby and don't want us around any more.'

'Edie!' Frances gave her sister a shocked look. 'You mustn't call her that. It's very wicked and now you'll have to ask God for forgiveness in your prayers.'

'Shan't!' said Edie, defiantly kicking at a stone in the road. The road was covered in stones and there were no pavements, only some wooden boards running down one side. There were no cars of course. Just a few piles of horse manure which Miss Dora waved them around, wrinkling up her nose with disgust. As Lily looked around her she realised she knew exactly where she was: they were in Cossins Place. She recognised the large bow windows and carved stone fronts. The Axteds' school was at Number 48, near the railway line. The houses were almost the same as in her time, except a bit cleaner perhaps. Lily was surprised to see that quite a lot were boarded up, with 'For Sale' notices outside. Then she noticed that the row of garages by the railway line was missing. In their place were some low stable buildings with horses' heads nodding over the doors.

'Please, Miss Dora, may we stroke the horses? Please!' Edie begged, opening her wide blue eyes beseechingly at her teacher.

Lily could see Miss Dora trying to think of a good reason why not, and failing. 'Alright girls, but please be careful they don't nibble your gloves. And don't be long, I don't wish to be late for luncheon.'

Edie rushed up and started stroking the head of a chocolate brown pony with a white streak on its forehead. 'This is my favourite. I call him Star. He pulled the trap for Number 12 before they sold him.'

'That's Rose's horse!' cried Lily, before she could stop herself. She'd been quite jealous of Rose's tales about her pony, but then sorry for her when she'd said how sad she'd been to lose him when her dad went bankrupt.

Edie was giving Lily a curious look. 'How do you know that? You said you only came from Leeds yesterday.'

'I, erm, overheard the servants talking,' Lily stuttered lamely. She could tell Edie wasn't convinced by this explanation. 'Which is your favourite, Frances?' she asked quickly, anxious to change the subject.

Frances pointed to a large, black stallion who was shaking his head and whinnying. 'That one, he's so noble-looking. I call him Alfonso.'

Edie giggled. 'Frances is in love with King Alfonso of Spain. He's the youngest king in Europe and she thinks he's *so* handsome. She even keeps a picture of him under her pillow!'

Frances blushed furiously and stamped over to Miss Dora. 'Can we move on now Miss Dora? I think we've seen enough of the horses.'

They turned out of Cossins Place onto the main road. Normally Lily would have expected to see queues of cars and buses, grinding their way up the steep hill from the city below. Today she stood and gasped in amazement. A sea of fields rolled away in front of her, broken only by the odd cottage and, in the far distance, a lone church spire. She stared up and down the stony track in front of her, trying to get her bearings. Right at the top of the hill she could see the pale, stone mansion of the Girls High School and beyond that, a few more large houses that she thought she recognised. Although in her time they'd been squashed in amongst a load of other buildings. Below her the railway line cut through high banks, and on the other side of the tracks was a park that definitely looked familiar…

'Come along now Lily, no dawdling. And do close your mouth or you'll catch a chill.'

Lily thought this was quite unlikely. She was already sweating under her layers of clothing. But she meekly followed Miss Dora over the road and down a small lane overgrown with blackberry and elder bushes.

I'm really here, she thought. I'm really here in 1898. I must try and remember everything, so when I'm back to my own time I can surprise everyone with how much I know about Victorian times.

She imagined winning a history prize at school and then appearing on TV. The presenter would be astounded by this child genius. 'It's almost as if you'd been there, Lily!'

Her daydreaming was brought to an abrupt halt by a terrible screech from Edie. She clutched at Lily's coat, her huge blue eyes full of terror and pointed into the bushes. The rotting remains of what had once been a badger were lying under the hedge. Lily could quite clearly see little white maggots crawling under the flesh.

'All God's creatures,' muttered Miss Dora, shooing them on past the corpse.

'I bet that's Mr Pike's doing,' said Frances, turning to Lily. 'He's the blacksmith who lives in the cottage down the stream. He thinks badgers spread disease and he's always setting traps for them.'

Miss Dora took them over a small wooden footbridge. Ahead of them there was a sagging shack with loud bangings and cursings coming out of it.

'He's awfully bad tempered,' giggled Edie. She stopped to peer into the gloomy doorway just as a shower of sparks blew out and made her jump back shrieking. 'It's just like Hell in there – all red and fiery!'

'Edith!' Miss Dora and Frances chorused, but Edie took no notice and skipped on up the path. Miss Dora tried to ignore her and turned to Lily. 'This stream is Cutlers Mill Brook and we will go back via Joe Goards wood. Try and remember the names. We shall be drawing a map of our *local* area in our next geography lesson, as it appears the wider world remains a mystery to you.'

Lily thought this was a bit unfair and wondered if she should tell her about her A-star rivers project. But there didn't seem to be a way she could do this without giving herself away, so she kept her mouth shut and looked hurt.

'Is that a sulky look I see on your face, Lily? There is nothing Our Lord hates more than a sulky child.'

Lily opened her mouth to disagree, but one look at Miss Dora's face made her snap it shut again. Really, she thought to herself, teachers here are always criticising and telling you off. It's impossible to do anything right, ever! She thought of how lovely her own teacher was at Phil and Jim. When I get back I'm going to be *so* helpful in the classroom and I promise I'll never moan about homework again…

They had come out of the woods and into a field dotted with jet black cows, munching their way through the thick grass.

'Ooh, I love those cows!' Edie ran ahead and pulled a fistful of green stalks which she waved over at the animals.

Miss Dora turned pale. 'Edith, stop that now! I've told you before not to encourage them.'

'Miss Dora's terrified of cows,' whispered Frances. 'And I know Edie loves animals, but I do think she's doing this just to give Miss Dora a fright.'

The cows had started lumbering towards them.

A bead of sweat appeared on Miss Dora's upper lip. 'Girls, follow me now please. I…' The last bit of her sentence was lost as she disappeared over the brow of the hill. Lily wouldn't have believed it was possible to move so fast in a long skirt and button boots. The girls trudged up the hill after her, Edie looking decidedly smug.

'The cows come all the way from Ireland, you know. Annie told me. They bring them up from the docks so they can have a last good feed before they're taken off to market.'

Lily frowned. 'You know what happens then, don't you?' She couldn't stop herself. 'They all have their throats cut and die – just so you can eat meat. That's why *I'm* a vegetarian.'

Edie and Frances gazed at her in horror. 'A *vegetarian*! You mean you don't eat meat at all? What on earth are you going to do at lunchtime?'

Chapter Seventeen

The Boy In The Garden

Lily was sitting at the dining room table. She felt sick with nerves. How was she going to tell the Miss Axteds that she didn't eat meat? Perhaps it would be cauliflower cheese? Or perhaps they wouldn't mind after all? But somehow she just knew they would. The maid brought in a silver soup tureen and placed it in front of Miss Axted who removed the lid with a flourish.

'Ah, kidney soup, delicious! Thank you, Betsy, I'll serve it out.'

Lily's stomach heaved and she thought she might actually be sick. She could see Edie and Frances looking at her nervously. Mrs Axted doled out a portion of the evil-smelling brown liquid and thrust it towards her.

It was now or never. Lily took a deep breath. 'Please Mrs Axted, did my Dad – I mean Papa – did he tell you that I'm a…um…vegetarian?'

Mrs Axted stopped spooning out the soup and turned slowly round to stare at Lily. 'No, he did not!' She glared at Lily as if she'd told her she was a mass murderer.

Miss Dora, looking flustered and dabbing at her mouth with

her napkin, broke the silence. 'Oh dear! This is quite unacceptable. We would never have agreed to take you if we'd known. We can't possibly expect Cook to serve up food especially for you.'

'I'll just eat the vegetables,' begged Lily. 'You don't need to go to any special trouble. Perhaps I could just have some cheese.'

Mrs Axted went purple. 'Cheese! Cheese! The child thinks she shall have *cheese*, on top of all her other expenses!'

Miss Mary patted her mother's arm. 'There, there, Mother, don't take on so. We'll write to Lily's father and ask for extra funds to cover the inconvenience. Have a little soup, mother dear. It's your favourite.'

Reluctantly Mrs Axted returned to her soup. But she continued to glower over at Lily, sniffing incredulously between gulps.

'Vegetarianism! Who ever heard of a child being a vegetarian? These newfangled ideas! Your father will regret it when you grow up weak and feeble. And you'll never find a husband willing to put up with that sort of nonsense!'

Lily lowered her head and tried to block out Mrs Axted's rantings. She imagined the harsh words sliding over the top of her head, whilst she daydreamed of summer holidays and ice cream. She'd had plenty of practice of doing this when she was being teased by the other kids at school.

The next course was no better. She was served a pile of slushy cabbage and potatoes. And that was all she got for lunch. I hope I don't die of malnutrition before I get back home, thought Lily. I wonder how long a person can survive without any real protein?

After lunch Miss Mary let them out into the back garden. 'But no running or jumping, just a quiet perambulation around the paths. I don't want you to give yourselves indigestion.'

Lily had been looking forward to seeing the garden. But when they trooped out of the kitchen door she was quite disappointed. Most of the garden was taken up by a large potting shed. Then there were some rows of vegetables and a scabby-looking apple tree. She could only see one patch of worn grass and that had old furniture piled up on it. There really was practically nowhere to play. And nothing to play with, not even a ball. Frances and Edie had linked arms and were walking slowly up and down chatting to each other. Lily felt suddenly left out and lonely. If only Rose was here, she found herself wishing. She'd got used to being the two of them. She'd forgotten what it was like to be all by herself. A sudden crack on the back of her head made her whisk around. Who on earth was throwing stones at her?

'I've been watching you for ages. You're new here aren't you?' A small boy with very red hair was crouched on top of the wall, half hidden by a laurel bush. 'Sorry about the stone. I tried a twig but it wouldn't go far enough.'

Lily rubbed the top of her head. 'Are you allowed up there? It's really high.'

'Father says we must experience a bit of danger in our lives or we'll grow up to be 'mice not men'. He's a theosophist you know.'

'What's a thosopist?' Lily was amazed that such a small boy knew such a big word.

'Well, it means we believe in lots of different Gods and we don't think we really die, we keep being born again as different things. And each time you come back, it gives you a chance to behave better.'

Lily thought for a bit. 'It sounds a bit like Buddhism. My mum was into that for a bit, but she couldn't cope with all the meditating. You're meant to not think of anything when you do it, but she kept thinking of shopping lists and what to have for tea. So she had to give it up.'

The small boy was now teetering on the edge of the wall.

'I really don't think you should do that,' Lily warned. 'I don't suppose your mum would like it, even if your dad wouldn't mind.'

'Oh alright,' he crouched back down again. 'Mother's really upset at the moment because my little brother died. Oh, you don't have to be sorry,' – he'd seen Lily's stricken expression – 'Father says he's just gone through a gateway into' – here he put on a solemn grownup voice – 'a fuller and more radiant existence.'

There was something very funny about the way he said this and they both started giggling, before Lily stopped herself.

'I'm sorry, I didn't mean to laugh. I am really sorry about Horace.'

'That's alright.'

But Lily noticed he was staring very hard at the ground and his lip was beginning to tremble.

'I don't really care about his next life you know. I'd just like him back in this one. My other brother's got it as well – the diphtheria thing. Father's sent him to a fever hospital so the rest of us don't catch it.'

'How many of you are there?' Lily loved the idea of big families.

'Well, there's me – I'm Neville. I'm the second oldest. Aubrey's the oldest – he's the one who's gone off to the fever hospital. Clarence and Wilfred are next after me and then there's Horace…' Neville stopped suddenly and stared hard at Lily. 'Why are you talking to me anyway? Haven't the Axeheads told you not to? We're 'Godless heathens' you know.'

Lily looked anxiously over her shoulder. She didn't want to get into any more trouble. There was no sign of the Axteds but she could see Edie and Frances waving at her from the other end of the garden.

'I better go. I think it's time to go in.'

'Alright then.' Neville turned and jumped off his side of the wall, disappearing instantly out of sight.

Lily walked over towards the other girls. She could tell from Frances's face she was going to get a warning about the 'heathens' next door.

Afternoon lessons were taken by Miss Mary Axted, the oldest and scariest of the sisters. Lily was nervous. She'd taken Dora to the limit with her lack of knowledge, how on earth would she manage with Miss Mary?

'Well, girls, as you know I attend the 'Lectures for Ladies' every week in the Clifton reading rooms. This afternoon I have decided to share with you some fascinating facts from one of those lectures. It was given by the eminent Professor Augustus Fieldhorn and is all about our local history.'

Lily's heart sank. This sounded horrendously boring. Miss Mary stared hard at Lily, as if she could tell what she was thinking, and then started speaking in a dramatic voice. 'Close your eyes, girls! I want you to forget for a moment that you are sitting here in our modern dining room. Instead I want you to think about the earth, just a few feet below you. Only a few years ago it would have been ploughed by farmers and trodden on by cattle. Before that Roman soldiers marched on it as they made their way to the port at Sea Mills. Maybe they sat and rested here in our garden. Maybe they dropped a coin or a ring for us to find. Let us cast our minds back even further. Right back, hundreds, thousands, millions of years. Now, beneath your feet, lap the warm waters of a tropical sea, full of strange and extraordinary creatures. Coral reefs grow here. For a short while they flower, then die – killed by the freezing waters that sweep down from the polar ice caps. As we travel back towards our own time, layer upon layer of rocks are laid down above the dying reefs – the very rocks that are then used to build this house!'

Lily shivered. Her eyes were squeezed shut, her mind full of images of exotic fish, warm seas, ancient stones – and time racing backwards and forwards. Miss Mary was a brilliant teacher. The hour's lesson flew by and by the end Lily wanted to beg her to carry on.

The next lesson did not go so smoothly. It was handwriting and Miss Mary was appalled by Lily's attempts to copy pages from, what Lily thought, was a very dull book about manners.

'What is this dreadful scrawl? I declare a spider has got into your inkwell and then walked all over the page! Did your governess not teach you to write in copperplate? This looks like the hand of a common workman!'

Glancing over at Frances's beautiful curly letters, Lily could see her own were rubbish in comparison. She hung her head, unable to think of any excuse that Miss Mary would have believed. Her punishment was to stay in after Edie and Frances were dismissed and write out rows and rows of wiggly *I*'s and *E*'s. When she was at last allowed to go up and join them, the sisters looked up at her sympathetically.

'Don't worry, there was another girl who came here who was even worse at lessons than you. She'd had some kind of brain fever,' Edie said comfortingly.

'What happened to her?'

'Oh she didn't last long. The Miss Axteds made her family take her back. Maybe they'll do the same to you if you're bad enough. I wish they'd send me back – only the Witch wouldn't take me of course...'

'Edie! You mustn't talk about Papa's wife like that. God hears everything, remember and you won't go to Heaven and see Mama again if you have wicked thoughts.' Frances looked severely down at her little sister, who just stuck her lower lip out and shrugged her shoulders.

Lily looked around the bare, cheerless room. 'Do you have any books, or games to play with?'

Frances shook her head. 'We used to have spillikins but Edie dropped them down the stairs onto Mrs Axted's head. She promised it was an accident but they confiscated them anyway.'

Lily could see Edie grinning behind Frances' back – somehow she didn't think it had been an accident.

'What about cards?'

'Oh no!' Both sisters shook their heads furiously. '*They* think card games are the work of the Devil. We do have those three books,' Frances pointed to some well worn volumes at one end of an otherwise empty bookshelf. 'But Edie and I have read them so many times they're almost falling apart. Papa sends us new ones on our birthdays, but the Miss Axteds never think they're 'suitable' and they throw them away.'

Lily was shocked at the thought of grownups throwing books away. 'So what do you do when you've got free time?'

'We make up stories and plays. Then we act them out, very quietly, so we don't disturb them downstairs. If we make a noise they come up and make us sit on our beds in silence and that's so boring!' Edie bounced up and down on the double bed she shared with her sister. Lily felt terrible for them. If they only knew how many toys and games she had in her room at home! She imagined how astonished they'd be by the Telly and computer games. No wonder Rose had got addicted to the Chuckles! She went over to the shelf and picked up the first volume on it. It was a small red book with golden daffodils embossed on the spine. It had a strange title. It was called *'Froggy's Little Brother'*. She opened it and started to read.

> *In the Neighbourhood of Shoreditch, a part of the East End of London inhabited mostly by very poor, hard working people, and seldom visited by the grand West End folk, there lived some years ago a Father and Mother and two little boys. The Father had a Punch and Judy show, which supported the family and kept them all employed except little Benny, the baby boy. The other little lad was named Tommy, but his Father always called him Froggy, because he was so often cold and croaked sometimes when he had a cough, like those little creatures who live in ditches and have such very wide mouths and large goggle eyes.*

'That's Edie's favourite book,' commented Frances. 'She loves it so much because it makes her cry buckets. The first time she read it she wept all night and soaked the back of *my* nightdress right through with her tears.'

Edie nodded seriously. 'Everybody dies by the end. *Everybody*. His mother. His father. His little brother. Even the mouse who was their only playmate...' She began to look tearful, her lower lip trembling.

'So what do they die of?' asked Lily.

'Well, his father gets knocked down by a cab. His mother gets phewmonia...'

'Pneumonia,' corrected Frances.

'Yes. And Benny gets 'the staggers'.'

'What on earth are 'the staggers'?' Lily looked puzzled.

'I'm not quite sure. But I think it's what Mr Cox's horse died of.'

'No it's not, Edie!' Frances and Edie started to argue about what the horse had died of and Lily decided to put the book away. It sounded way too sad and way too full of alarming deaths.

'Lets play charades. Do you know that game?'

They did, but it proved more difficult than Lily had expected. The sisters kept choosing scenes from the Bible, or Greek plays that she'd never heard of. And of course it was very hard for her to think of titles that *they* would know.

'I've got one!' Lily mimed out the words for *Alice in Wonderland*. Edie started jumping up and down.

'I know it! It's that book Mama used to read us at bedtime. The funny one with the cat and the white rabbit – you know the one I mean Francie!'

But Frances didn't reply. She was staring down at the bedspread, picking at some loose threads and looking very sad.

'Edith! What is the meaning of this terrible racket?' Miss Mary stood in the doorway, glaring down at them.

Lily sighed to herself. It was so easy to get shouted at here and so difficult to do anything right. It made her long for a big hug from her own mum. A wave of homesickness washed over her. How much longer did she have to stay in this ghastly house? She'd thought travelling in time would be fun. A big adventure. She hadn't imagined it would mean impossible lessons, endless praying, and being told off all the time.

I mustn't be selfish, she thought. I must think about Aubrey and how I'm going to help him. Did I really swap places with him? Did it actually work? And how will I know when to go back? But Lily didn't have time to puzzle for long: her thoughts were interrupted by Mary, ordering them downstairs for 'supper'.

Lily was starving. It seemed ages since her plate of cabbage at lunchtime. But she was horribly disappointed when she saw the meal laid out for them – just a pile of cold toast and a glass of water. No wonder Frances and Edie looked so thin and pale. She wolfed her portion down and considered asking for more, like Oliver Twist. But she could just guess what the Axteds would think of that! So she kept quiet and tried to stop her stomach from rumbling too loudly.

The unsatisfactory meal was followed by more prayers. After which bedtime came as a relief. She was tired of trying to please the Axteds and at least she couldn't do anything wrong in bed. Even though it was early – only 6.30pm – Lily was exhausted. She heard whisperings from the big bed in the corner. Then a whinny from one of the horses in the stables down the road, followed by a crunch of footsteps on the gravel drive next door. Then nothing.

CHAPTER EIGHTEEN

A Telegram And A Music Lesson

Before Lily opened her eyes the next morning, she wished. She wished she was back in her pink bedroom at home, with her clothes piled up on the floor and her mum banging about in the kitchen downstairs. But instead she felt the same stiff cotton sheets as yesterday and when she breathed in, the taste of coal dust caught in the back of her throat and made her cough. Outside she could the sound of a man calling. 'Whoah, Bluebell. Wheya now, Maisie!'

There was a deep mooing and shuffling of hooves from outside the window. Lily stifled her disappointment and pulled back the thin curtains to stare out into the street.

There was a patter of little feet as Edie pushed in besides her. 'Look!' Edie pointed to a procession of cows swaying their way down the road. 'They're the cows from up on the Green. I know all their names – Bluebell, Star, Gertrude, Emily, Belle, Trixie…'

'Maisie – I heard the man call her,' put in Lily.

'What do you want to be when you grow up?' Edie asked, with one of her lightening changes of subject.

'I want to be a Professor of History. It's my best subject at school. Or an archaeologist, digging up lost cities and finding out what people used to eat. That sort of thing.'

Edie looked surprised. 'No, I mean *really* what do you want to do – you can't do any of those things 'cos you're a girl. *I'm* going to run an orphanage in an enormous house in the country. There'll be a huge garden where you can play whenever you like. And no lessons. They'll have lovely new clothes… Oh yes! And there'll be pink iced buns for tea everyday!'

'You're just being silly, Edie. There would have to be lessons or how would they learn to read and write? And where would you get the money for all those clothes and buns?' Frances was sitting up in bed, rubbing her eyes and frowning.

'No, you're the silly, Frances! I'm going to marry a very rich man. He'll probably be away at sea a lot, so I'll look after the orphans by myself.'

'Well, I shall *never* get married,' declared Frances. 'It's not fair on your children if you die and they get left with a horrible stepmother.'

'Ooh, Frances! You said we shouldn't say rude things about the Witch!'

''Witch' is much worse Edie. Now do be quiet, it's only 5.30 in the morning – we should all go back to sleep.'

The long day passed in much the same way as the previous one. Only this time Lily got to show how bad she was at French verbs and to fail dismally in a Scripture test. Edie spent more time in the corner – after refusing to eat a single spoonful of the vile porridge – and lunch arrived with all the vegetables soaked in rich, meaty gravy. Mrs Axted watched with fury as Lily tried to scrape the sauce of her potatoes.

'How you can turn your nose up at perfectly good food, I shall never know. You are a growing girl and the Good Lord tells us in the Bible that we may feast upon his creatures. I consider it *blasphemous* to deny his Word.'

Pudding was gooseberry tart, which would have been nice if they'd been allowed some of the sugar that the Axteds heaped on theirs. Edie pulled terrible faces as the sour fruit hit her tongue, and then once again ended up back in the corner. Lily was so ravenous she forced all of hers down. But she still left the table feeling hungry.

Things got better after lunch when Miss Mary entranced the girls with a talk on Astronomy. 'This afternoon girls, I want to tell you about Dr Clement Devereaux, Royal Astronomer to the Queen. His discoveries have astounded scientists all over the world and he is beginning to unlock the very secrets of the universe itself.'

Lily felt a shiver travel up and down her spine, there was a magical quality to Mary's voice that made her skin tingle.

'He has seen galaxies far beyond our own. Found new suns and moons and stared deep into the mysteries of space!' Mary kept them fascinated for the full hour of the lesson, although Lily wasn't sure if *everything* she told them was correct. She seemed very sure there were little green men on Mars and she told Edie off for suggesting humans might one day fly to the moon.

Lily wished she could shout out, *They will! They really will. I know. I've seen it!* But of course she kept quiet – she didn't want Mary to think she was mad and cart her off to some awful Victorian lunatic asylum.

Their walk that morning took them to the park on the other side of the railway track. Lily could just about recognise it as Cotham Gardens. Instead of being in the middle of town, it now looked out over farms and fields and half the city seemed to have disappeared. All the play equipment had vanished and in their place there were paths and flower beds. Only the railway was unchanged, running along the park's northerly edge and off towards the distant hills. Some small, overdressed children in big hats stood by the railings, ready to wave at passing trains, just like Lily used to when she was little. The Axteds did not approve of playing and, in fact, it would have been difficult to do much because they were so trussed up in their outdoor clothes. They sat in the shade on a park bench, with Mary and Dora nodding and saying 'Hello' to passers-by. Edie pleaded with them to go for a walk and eventually they gave in. 'As long as you stay together and don't go out of our sight.'

Frances linked arms with Lily, which was nice. It was the first friendly touch she'd had since she'd arrived in their time. They walked past boys and girls, bowling hoops and playing hopscotch – some of them looked quite jolly and carefree. Lily guessed not all Victorian children lived lives as strict and dull as they did at the Axteds'. She stopped suddenly and pointed at a slight, dark haired child in a black dress. 'Who's that?'

The girl was some way away from them, but there was something oddly familiar about her. Lily felt a shiver, almost as though she'd seen a ghost. Where had she seen her before? She felt sure she knew her from somewhere.

Frances glanced over. 'Oh, that's Rose Cox. She must be back from the seaside. Her mother sent her away because of the diphtheria.

They must have decided it was alright for her to come home now.'

That's not Rose Cox! Lily wanted to blurt out, but she managed to bite her tongue just in time. Of course! That must be Rose Perkins, the girl from Peru. Lily stared at her. She was so like the Rose she knew, but at the same time not like her. Her hair wasn't as dark, and the shape of her face wasn't quite right. Should she go over and talk to her? But what would she say? Would it be, in some way, against the rules to make contact with her? The girl looked happy enough, she was chatting energetically to a pleasant-looking, young woman who was sitting next to her. If she *was* Rose Perkins she didn't look at all upset by her time travelling.

Frances was pulling at her arm. 'Come *on*, Lily! Let's see how Victoria's oak is doing, shall we?' But Edie continued to gaze at the girl, and then turned her large, blue eyes inquisitively back to Lily.

Lily turned away abruptly and followed Frances up the slope to where the massive tree should have been. It was nowhere to be seen.

Frances didn't seem at all surprised. 'It's doing very well now,' she said, as she patted the earth around the roots of a spindly sapling. 'Look, Edie it's nearly up to your waist.' Edie had joined them, although she was still looking rather oddly at Lily. The young tree was just poking up above the shiny new metal milestone. 'We came here for the ceremony last year,' Frances continued, 'It was planted for the Queen's Diamond Jubilee.'

'And they lit up the suspension bridge with lanterns. All the way across!' Edie interrupted. 'But the Axheads wouldn't take us to see it, though I begged and begged! Did you know?' Edie carried on, with another of her rapid changes of subject. 'The Queen's really old now, so she'll die soon and we'll have to wear black. And so the Axteds will *have* to buy us new dresses – whether they like it or not!'

'Edie, you mustn't talk about her Majesty like that. If someone overheard you, you could be arrested for treason!' Frances frowned. 'It will be odd though. To have a King instead of a Queen. Nobody can remember what that's like, it's been so long. I don't suppose there'll ever be a Queen who reigns as long as ours ever again.'

Lily wanted to blurt out *yes there will! She'll reign just as long and she'll be called Elizabeth the Second – just wait and see!* But of course she didn't, she felt that would be against the rules. Whatever the rules were. Somehow she knew Mrs F would disapprove if she did. And although she *seemed* like a nice old woman, she was also a pretty powerful one too.

After a while the days at 'The Misses Axteds' Establishment for Young Ladies' seemed to blend into one another. Every part of the day was tightly controlled. Lily very rarely had any time to herself. She was often bored – particularly during the endless prayer sessions – and always hungry. But after a while she found she was getting used to the predictability of her new life. She never had to make any decisions; that was all done for her. And there were no choices to be made: the Axteds told her exactly what to do and how to do it. The part of the day she looked forward to the most was the precious 'free time' up in their room. Frances was brilliant at making up plays and Edie was often excruciatingly funny. Sometimes they'd have to stuff socks in their mouths to muffle their laughter from the Axteds in the drawing room below. Lily realised she was thinking about her own time less and less

– even her own mum – and that frightened her. *I mustn't forget my old life*, she told herself, *I might miss my chance to get back and I don't want to be stuck here forever!*

On the fifth day – or was it the sixth? Lily was having difficulty keeping count – the girls were gathered in the hall pulling on their hats and gloves, when there was a sharp rap on the door. Without thinking, Lily, who was closest to it, pulled the door open. A spotty teenage boy with a funny, little round hat perched on his head was standing there, holding out a piece of paper. He thrust it at Lily, turned smartly around and shot off down the drive.

Lily had just enough time to close the door before Miss Dora appeared. 'Did I hear someone at the door? You know you must never answer the door without permission.'

Without knowing quite why she did it, Lily slipped the telegram into her pocket. 'It wasn't anybody. I thought I heard something but it must have been the wind.'

Frances and Edie looked at Lily aghast. Lying was about the worst sin you could commit in the Axteds' school. She knew they wouldn't tell on her, but she would have to think up a really good story to explain why she'd hidden the note. Which would be tricky, as she didn't really know herself.

Much to Dora's surprise, Lily took a sudden interest in the wild flowers they passed on their walk. Lily knew this was one of her teacher's favourite subjects, so she nodded enthusiastically as Dora explained their Latin names and why they grew in particular places along the lane. It kept her out of the way of Frances and Edie, who had heard it all before and were deliberately hanging back to avoid the lecture. Lily waited until Dora was distracted by Edie, who was kicking at stones in the road. Then she hurriedly pulled the card out of her pocket. What she read made her sick with fright.

DEAR MRS AXTED STOP DAUGHTER NOT VEGETARIAN STOP HAS THERE BEEN CONFUSION OVER DATES STOP SHE IS DUE TO ARRIVE 18TH JUNE STOP

Trembling Lily stuffed it back in her pocket: the 18th of June was tomorrow!

Half an hour later they were trudging back up Cossins Place. As they approached Number 48, Miss Dora pointed to a black silk umbrella, leaning against the front door.

'Ah, I see Mamselle has arrived for your singing class. Hurry along girls – you must be punctual for her.'

They wriggled out of their outdoor things and Lily could tell by the sisters' faces that this was one lesson they were really looking forward to. It was the first time Lily had been into the drawing room at the front of the house. It was where the Axteds sat when the girls were banished upstairs to their bedroom. Despite the large bay window, the room was very dark. The sunlight was shut out by thick velvet drapes and yellowed net curtains. Gas lamps spluttered on either side of the grey marble fireplace and in their dim orange glow, Lily could see the room was crammed with furniture. There were ornate chairs and couches, little tables and cabinets, bookcases and desks. Every surface was covered in a sea of ornaments and photo frames. Lily couldn't help stepping nearer to peer at these.

One showed a chubby young man with floppy hair and a large moustache. His foot was resting on the body of a stripy tiger, and there was a rather unpleasant grin on his face. Scrawled across the front of the photo were the words: *One for the pot, Ay Sis?*

That's got to be Reggie, Lily thought.

Most of the pictures seemed to be of him. There he was in tennis whites, holding an odd, oval-shaped racket. Then again, posing in black tie and tails with a cigar sticking out the side of his mouth. Next as a schoolboy in blazer and cap. And finally as a fat child in a sailor suit, clutching a toy gun.

'Vell, vell Lily here ve are again.'

Lily swung round. An old woman was standing in the shadows. She was wearing a long, black crinkly dress and a strange little lace cap. As she stepped forward into the pool of yellow gas light, her dark eyes bore straight into Lily's. Then, abruptly, she turned and clapped her hands. 'Edith, Frances! My little song birds. Let us begin the lesson. Ve vill begin with a polka, I think.'

The sisters looked at their music teacher adoringly. 'She *never* gets cross or tells us off,' Edie whispered to Lily.

Lily tripped and stumbled her way through the complicated dance steps, expecting at any minute to be told how badly she was doing. But Mamselle just nodded kindly at her.

'Vy don't you sit out for this one, leetle Lily. You can vatch the others and learn from them, yes?'

Relieved, Lily plumped down into one of the big armchairs. For a while she watched Edie and Frances glide gracefully around the furniture, then her eyes wandered over to the mantelpiece which was stuffed with knick-knacks and yet more photos. One in particular caught her eye: it showed three little girls, dressed in layers of frothy petticoats. They were sitting in a row their little, booted legs hanging over the edge of the photographer's couch. The oldest one was leaning forwards slightly with a serious expression, but the younger two were very obviously giggling, the youngest one so much so that her ringleted head was thrown back, blurring the print. Lily could just imagine their mother sighing and saying, 'Well, it will just have to do. We'll never get them to all sit still at once!' But what really amazed her was how alive they looked, as if they might jump out of the frame and start running around the room. And there was something familiar about their faces. Of course! The older one was Mary, she recognised the high forehead and frown. The middle child was Dora and the laughing baby must be Annie – the sister who was visiting the sick aunt in Bath.

How odd, thought Lily, that they were children just like us. And that they were naughty and laughed when they were supposed to be serious for the camera. Why don't they *remember* what it was like to be a child and want to have fun? Why are they *always* telling us off?

'Now girls, ve vill do some singing. Something simple that even Lily vill know.' Mamselle glanced over at Lily with her liquorice-black eyes – and did she wink? Lily got up, feeling confused. There was something about the old lady that made her feel sure they'd met before, if only she could remember where.

> *Row, row, row your boat,*
> *Gently down the stream,*
> *Merrily, merrily, merrily, merrily,*
> *Life is but a dream.*

Lily closed her eyes and let the tune flow over her. She used to sing this song with her mum on long car journeys and it always made her feel safe and dreamy. For the first time in ages she let herself think about home: her mum, her bedroom, buying sweets on Chandos Road. Chandos Road! The wool shop! Mrs F – that's who Mamselle reminded her of. Except this lady seemed older and greyer. She opened her eyes and saw the old lady, nodding at her and smiling. She knows I've recognised her, thought Lily, and smiled shyly back.

'When are we going to do 'Oranges and Lemons'? You *know* it's my favourite, can we do it now, *please*!' Edie was hopping about looking pleadingly at her teacher.

'Vell, vell, we shall haf to call you 'Little Miss Impatience', shan't we?' Mrs F pretended to frown at the little girl, but it was obvious she wasn't really annoyed, not like the Axteds would be.

'Can I be the big bell at Bow?' Edie beamed up at her.

'Of course. Always my leetle one. Now let's begin!'

Lily loved the music lesson. They sang *Greensleeves, The Sky Boat Song* and finished off with *What Shall We Do with the Drunken Sailor*, which gave Edie lots of opportunity to show off her glugging and staggering about. At the end of the class Mrs F asked Lily to stay behind and help put the furniture back in place.

'So we meet again, Lily.' She wasn't talking in a foreign accent any more, she sounded just like she had in the shop on Chandos Road.

'I've got to get back!' blurted out Lily. 'The real Lily – I mean the Lily who was supposed to be coming here – is arriving tomorrow! Then the Axteds will know I'm a fraud and they'll probably kick me out or call the police, or worse!'

Mrs F looked perfectly calm. 'I know. All will be well. You have till tomorrow to work out what to do, and that will be plenty of time.'

Lily gawped at her in amazement. 'No it won't! And no, I don't –have a clue what to do I mean. Can't you just tell me? After all it is kind of your fault I'm here, making me time travel and stuff!' Lily found herself getting quite angry and forgetting all her Victorian manners about not answering back to adults. Mrs F looked at her for a long time, a sad expression on her lined, old face.

'Is it not for Aubrey that you are here, little one? Is it not to help save a life?'

Lily instantly felt dreadful. Of course it was. And here she was just being horribly selfish and worrying about herself, while Aubrey might be out there dying. Mrs F's expression softened, as if she could read Lily's mind.

'Did you not tell Rose you would try to contact her somehow?'

'Yes. Yes I did.'

'Well now is the time to do it. You will find a way tonight. Don't worry, Lily, you have all the strength and courage you need – you just don't realise it yet.' She placed a stiff black bonnet on her head and began tying the ribbon under her chin. 'All will be well, Lily. All will be well'.

CHAPTER NINETEEN

The Boy On The Roof

That evening at supper Lily kept coughing and clearing her throat loudly. The Axteds tried to ignore her, so she put her head in her hands and started moaning until, at last, they were forced to take notice.

'What is the meaning of this performance, Lily?' Mrs Axted scowled down the table, furious that her meal had been interrupted by her least favourite pupil.

'Please Ma'am, I don't feel very well. I think it's my throat.' Lily clutched at her neck dramatically. Miss Dora gave a sharp intake of breath and all of them, even old Mrs Axted, looked concerned. Mary looked at her intently.

'I think you should go up to your room and lie down. It's probably just a chill. I noticed you forgot to take your gloves with you on your walk this morning. Run along now. Edie and Frances can sleep in Reggie's room tonight. We don't want them to catch anything.'

Gratefully, Lily sped out of the room and up the stairs. Behind her she could hear Mrs Axted, complaining loudly. 'Well I shan't be calling the doctor out. It's far too expensive *and* her father still hasn't sent any money for her board. We're not running a charity here you know...'

Lily was delighted to be out of the stuffy dining room. Her plan had worked. The Axteds were worried that she might have diphtheria and she'd won some time by herself to work out her escape. She *had* to get back to her own time by tomorrow, or the real Lily from Leeds would turn up and blow her cover. That meant she had to contact Rose in order to swap back with Aubrey. But would Aubrey be well enough by now? Would Rose have found a way of getting him cured? He must be alright, she tried to reassure herself. Otherwise Mrs F wouldn't have turned up and told me 'all would be well'. She must know he's okay. It must be the right time. But, oh, how can I contact Rose? How can I get a message across time to tell her I need to come back?

She sat on the hard iron bed and tried to force the answers into her mind. Her brain felt fogged up with thinking and she pushed her face down into her knuckles until stars burst in front of her eyes. A note! Of course! I told her I would leave a message for her under the milestone tree. If I bury it carefully it could still be there in a hundred years. Couldn't it?

Lily sat up, feeling very pleased with herself. Mrs F was right. She did know what to do. The old oak was the perfect place to hide a message. But how on earth would she get to it? How could she get out of the house without being caught by the Axteds? I'll work that out in a minute, she thought. First I'll write the note and then I'll think what to do next. After all, I don't want to use up all my brain power at once.

Lily searched around the room. She found an old quill and a

pot of ink with a small amount of black liquid left in the bottom. But there was no paper. She went over to the bookcase and took down *Froggy's Little Brother*. 'Sorry, Edie', she whispered, as she tore out one of the blank pages from the back of the book. She leant against the mantelpiece, and had just begun to write, when she heard footsteps on the stairs outside her room. Hastily she scribbled the rest of the message,

> *17th June*
> *HELP! You must get me back NOW!!*
> *'L'*

She slid the paper into her pocket just as the door opened and Miss Dora swept in. 'How are you feeling now, Lily? I trust you are a little improved. Although you do appear slightly flushed.'

'I…er…I do feel a bit better Miss Dora. But, um, not quite right. I think if I had a lie down I'd feel much better.'

Dora nodded, looking relieved. 'Well, I don't think we need call out the doctor quite yet. God willing, it's not the diphtheria. Edie and Frances will sleep in Reggie's room for tonight and hopefully you will feel yourself again by the morning.'

Lily felt guilty for making her so anxious, but she had to keep up the pretence of being ill while she planned her next move. She wouldn't stand a chance of getting her message to the park if Edie and Frances were around. After Miss Dora had left the room she changed into her nightdress, then knelt up on her bed and stared out of the window. She was hoping that somehow an idea would just pop into her head.

Directly below her was the flat roof of the bay window. If I could climb down onto that, I'd be able to lower myself onto the lawn, she thought. If I waited until dark maybe I could run to the park and back without being seen. She heaved up the sash window and stuck her head out. She gulped. It was an awfully long way down and she'd make a terrible crash when she landed on the roof below. Someone would be bound to hear it.

'Hello there. You've gone to bed awfully early!'

Lily started. Where had that voice come from? She thought she recognised it, but couldn't think who it was. She peered around until she spotted a small figure high up on the roof next door. It was Neville, grinning and swinging his legs over the edge of the parapet.

'Do you always play in such dangerous places?'

'Yep,' Neville answered cheerfully. 'So why are you in bed *now*? It's not even six o'clock yet. Have you been really wicked? Did they send you to bed without any supper?'

'No, I've just been feeling a bit sick...' Lily started to explain, then stopped – seeing Neville had just given her a brainwave. 'Will you play a game? A really important game, that you mustn't tell the grownups about?'

'I can keep a secret. Aubrey and I had our own special code and I never told anyone – not even Clarence or Wilfred when they begged me to and sat on my head. But what's the game? I hope it's not a boring old girl's game.'

Lily felt a bit annoyed by that remark, but managed to bite her tongue. After all she had to keep Neville on her side. 'Come over here and I'll tell you. If you get down onto your bay window you can jump across. But try and do it quietly, I don't want the Axteds to hear.'

Neville scrambled down a drain pipe then leapt over, so he was standing just under Lily's window. 'Spill the beans then.'

'Promise you won't tell anyone?'

'Cross my heart and hope to die, shoot a squirrel in the eye.' Neville drew a cross over his heart and then spat over his right shoulder.

'Well, it's a game called 'Secret Messages'.' Lily was making it up as she went along, but she seemed to have captured Neville's attention, so she carried on. 'We leave a message in the park – I've already found the perfect spot by the milestone oak. Then, maybe in a hundred years or so, someone will dig it up and read our secret message!'

Neville looked disappointed. 'But we'll be dead by then, so we'll never know if it's been found.'

Lily thought quickly. '*You* may not be around, but what about your grandchildren? And great-grandchildren? Just think how exciting it would be if your grandfather had hidden a message for *you* to find!'

Neville looked unconvinced. 'Well I'm never getting married. Girls are too soppy, so I'll never have grandchildren.'

Lily sighed, how on earth could she persuade Neville to do what she wanted?

'It has to be done at night, in the dark, after everyone else is in bed. And you have to creep out without *anybody* knowing and run to the park and back. Perhaps you're too scared to do it?'

'No, of course I'm not! I'll do it. Though I still think it's a pretty stupid game, 'cos you never get to find out what happens in the end.' He thought a bit more and then added: 'Will you buy me some sweets for doing it?'

Lily's heart sank. She didn't want to make a promise she'd have to break. If everything worked out she'd be far away in time by the morning, with no chance of delivering sweets to Victorian boy over a hundred years earlier. 'Neville, what if I were to tell you there's an even bigger secret, *much* bigger than hiding a message in the park. But it's *so* secret I can't tell you without putting someone's life in danger – someone *very* close to you.' Lily was thinking on her feet, desperate not to give too much away, but also desperate to keep Neville involved.

He gave her a withering look. 'Well, why didn't you say so in the first place? Of course I will. Where's the note?'

Lily hung out of the widow holding the message in her finger tips. By standing on tiptoe Neville could just reach it. He took the paper and was about to unfold it when Lily hissed down at him.

'Don't! It's really important you don't read it. Will you promise not to?'

Neville crossed and spat again. 'Alright. But won't it go mouldy and crumble away? A hundred years is an awfully long time. I know! I've a little tin box I keep my soldiers in – that'll keep it dry. And stop the mice nibbling at it!'

Lily leaned over the sill and looked down at Neville's earnest face framed by his shock of orange hair. He was only a little boy and she felt guilty for making him go to the park at night, all by himself. But he had much more experience at climbing out of windows than her *and* he didn't have the Axteds to get past.

'Make sure you bury it in the right place – in front of the milestone tree. And not too close, because the tree's going to get much bigger in a hundred years time…'

But she was talking to thin air. Neville had already turned and slid over the side of the bay window. The last she saw of him was a flash of red hair as he jumped back over the wall into his own garden. Oh, I do hope he does it, I *really* hope he does it, Lily thought to herself. Then she yawned, all that thinking and planning had made her tired. She lay down and pulled the covers up over her head. She'd asked for help in the note and she'd put today's date on it. So if Rose got the note in time and Aubrey was well enough then they'd be wishing at some point tonight. She didn't dare think about what would happen if they didn't get her note, or Aubrey hadn't got better. Would she be stuck in this time for ever? She pushed the thought out of her head and squeezed her eyes tightly shut. They will get the note, they will, they *will*. And everything will be fine! I'll stay awake and wish every hour, holding my crystal. They're bound to wish on the hour. I'll be home this time tomorrow…

It was much harder to stay awake than Lily had imagined. She tried to read the Sunday Annual from the sister's book collection, but it was incredibly boring. There was a chapter on, 'How to do good deeds for poor folk'. And another called, 'Crochet your own prayer book cover'. She tried counting the daffodils on the wallpaper, but her eyelids kept drooping, and as dusk fell she couldn't see them to count any more. Her head started to nod forward onto her chest, then jerked up as she remembered she had to keep awake. Three times the long hand of the clock pointed to the hour and three times Lily clutched the sharp sides of the crystal and wished to return to her own time. But every time she opened her eyes she saw the same thin curtains and bare room.

'Lily!'

A small hand was shaking her awake. Lily struggled to open her eyes. It was pitch black in the room, but she could tell by the smell of coal and polish that she was still at the Axteds. Oh no! She *had* fallen asleep. What time was it now? Had she missed her chance to get back?

'Who's there?' she whispered.

'It's me of course, you silly.' Edie poked her face right up against Lily's.

'Uuh, I thought you and Frances were in Reggie's old room tonight.'

'We were,' said Edie triumphantly. 'But I escaped! I knew you weren't really sick. Frances is pretending to believe you but I know she's just saying that to annoy me. I crept over the landing as soon as I heard the Axteds go to bed. They're snoring like steam trains!'

'You must go back,' pleaded Lily. 'They mustn't find you in here. It's really important, Edie!'

Edie looked at her curiously. 'Why? Why is it so important? And why did you hide that telegram? Was it from your Papa?'

'Please Edie, don't ask questions – just go back to your room. It's really complicated, and you wouldn't understand.' As soon as she'd said this Lily realised her mistake. A look of furious stubbornness came over Edie's face.

'Oh yes, I would! I understand a lot more than you think. You think just because I'm younger than you that I'm silly and don't notice things. Well I do! I noticed you knew all about Rose Cox from up the road. You even knew the name of her horse. And

I noticed you never talked about Leeds or your family. *And* I noticed you were always asking questions and never seemed to know how to do things. You see, I notice lots of things that grown-ups don't!'

Lily felt a chill of fear go through her. Yes, she'd fooled the Axteds and even just about fooled Frances, but she hadn't fooled Edie. She'd seen all her mistakes. Would she tell? Lily stared through the gloom at Edie and saw with a shock that the little girl was crying.

'You're going away aren't you? That's what all this is about, isn't it? Oh how horrid – to go away without telling us. I thought we were friends!'

Lily hugged her. 'Yes, of course we're friends! You and Frances have been the best friends to me. But I do have to go away. I'm really, really sorry Edie, but I couldn't tell you because it's a secret – even the Axteds don't know I'm going – and I thought it was safer if I didn't tell you either. I didn't want you to get into trouble as well.'

Edie looked at her with her huge blue eyes full of tears. 'Take me with you, Lily. Please!'

'I can't, Edie – and even if I could, you wouldn't really leave Frances would you?'

Tears slid down Edie's face and dripped onto the collar of her long white nightie. 'I suppose it wouldn't be fair to go without her. But I *will* get away from this place one day – I will, I *will*!'

'I know you will!' Lily squeezed Edie tight.

'Can I stay with you – until you go? I won't tell a soul, I promise – even if they whip me and shut me in the cellar.'

Lily couldn't stop herself grinning. 'I don't think even the Axteds would go that far, Edie. But even so, it wouldn't be a good idea. Suppose Frances woke up and found you were gone? She might get scared and wake the Axteds up and then I mightn't get back to my own time...' Lily stopped. She hadn't meant to say that last bit.

Edie stepped back and stared into Lily's eyes: a long, deep stare that made her seem much older than her seven years. Then she nodded once, almost as if she'd understood what Lily had really meant.

'Remember me, won't you, Lily?'

Lily nodded back, she felt too choked to speak. Edie turned and the last Lily saw of her was the hem of her small nightdress disappearing around the door.

Lily looked at the clock. It was twelve o'clock exactly. Now! She clenched her fists around the crystal. Now! I want to go back now!

Chapter Twenty

Ward 17 And A Plane Ticket

Rose sat in the front room of Lily's house. She was watching TV, but it wasn't working its usual magic on her.

We are the Chuckles; we're here to make you smile. We are the Chuckles; come dance with us a while!

But Rose didn't feel like dancing or smiling just now, she was thinking about Lily's letter. That 'Now!' that Lily'd put at the end sounded so desperate – and the 17th of June was tomorrow, which meant she had roughly twenty four hours to come up with a rescue plan.

'Rose! Time for tea.' Sylvia called her through to the kitchen where she served up some pumpkin soup and knobbly bread.

Sylvia tried hard to make cheerful conversation, but she looked awfully worn and tired. Rose knew how worried she must be about Lily and felt horribly guilty for not telling her the truth about where she was. She also guessed it wouldn't be long before Sylvia rang the police to report Lily missing. It was yet another reason she had to get Lily back tomorrow.

'Mmm, lovely soup. Can I have another helping?'

'Yes, of course, dear,' Sylvia replied. But she was staring into space and didn't actually move to give her any more.

Rose tried again, 'Sylvia, have you heard from Dr Steele? Do you know how that boy's doing?'

Sylvia's face brightened up. 'Yes, sweetie, I do. Apparently he's doing marvellously, but he still has no memory of who he is or what he was he doing in the park. Richard said they're thinking of getting a hypnotist in to try and unlock his mind.'

Rose went rigid. Cook had told her about a hypnotist she'd seen at a fair up on the Downs. He'd convinced a grown man that he was a dog and made him crawl around on all fours while the crowd laughed at him. She didn't want that happening to Aubrey. And suppose it did unlock his mind and he told them where he really came from? Would they believe him? Or would they think he'd gone mad and lock him up in an asylum?

'I really want to visit him again, Sylvia. Please can we go after school?'

'I'm afraid not darling. I'm taking the stall to the Green Earth Fair in St Werburgh's and I won't be back in time. You've got the key haven't you? So you can let yourself in and if there's anything you need you can pop next door to the Steele's. I should be back around sixish.'

Rose's heart sank. Then it struck her. If Sylvia was out of the house it would be the perfect time to smuggle Aubrey in! All she had to do was get him out of the hospital and back here. Rose grinned to herself. This time she didn't feel even a twinge of guilt for deceiving Sylvia. 'Okay, Mrs Sta – I mean Sylvia – I'll be fine, don't worry!'

***

It was four o'clock the next day, the 17th of June, the day everything had to change and Rose was on her way up to the children's' hospital. Rose imagined them all lined up like chess pieces: Lily, Aubrey, Rose Perkins, herself. All ready to move in one last, fiendishly complicated, game. She knew Lily would be ready to wish. Her job was to get herself and Aubrey into place. Rose Perkins was the one piece she had no control over. She just had to hope that Mrs F would take care of that one. Then – if they all made the right move at the right time, check mate! Game over! All back to their own time.

If only she could be sure Rose Perkins would be ready. There had been nothing in Lily's note about contacting her. Could she really leave that move to chance and Mrs F? Rose suddenly changed direction; she had been heading up the hill to the hospital, but now she ran back down again. She turned right into Chandos Road, past the butcher's, the restaurants and the bakery, until, breathless, she arrived outside the dark blue entrance of the wool shop. Above the glass panels engraved with 'Personal Service' and 'Experienced Attention', there was a large, white board. On it was the word: 'SOLD'.

Rose banged on the door. There was no reply. She peered in through the windows, but they were blank and empty: no piles of wool, no knitting needles, no knitted gloves or bootees. But then she saw a movement, a shadow at the back of the shop; she started to bang on the glass and shout.

'Mrs F! Mrs F! It's me, Rose. Please answer the door. *Please*, it's very important!'

The shadow came forwards into the daylight at the front of the shop. It wasn't Mrs F, it was Maureen, her shop assistant. She opened the door with a familiar tinkle of the bell and looked down, concerned, at Lily's anxious face.

'What is it my, luvver? What's to do?'

'I…I wanted to speak to Mrs F. Is she here? It's really important.'

Maureen's forehead creased. 'I'm sorry, my duck, she's moved on. She said she was getting to old to run a shop. Although if you ask me she seemed to be getting younger every year!' Maureen laughed, but then seeing Rose's serious face she carried on. 'She's gone – oh what's the name of that place, our Miche?' She shouted back over her shoulder to her sister who appeared from the back of the shop, shaking out a duster.

'She never rightly said, Mor. She's what you might call a 'free spirit' – bought one of those fancy tents that sounds like a yoghurt, isn't that right, Mor?'

'Yurt I think they's called, Miche. Anyway she's off on her travels now. Miche and I are just tidying up, then it'll be let again – probably another restaurant or estate agent I shouldn't wonder. You alright sweetheart?'

'I'm fine. I was just hoping to see her one more time, but if she's not here I'll – I'll just have to manage by myself I suppose…' she trailed off, realising she was making no sense at all to the two women. 'Thank you for helping me. I better go now. Bye!' Rose raced off down the road leaving the two sisters looking curiously after her.

She puffed up the hill towards the children's hospital. She mustn't waste any more time; she had to get Aubrey back before Sylvia arrived home from the market. She tried not to feel too disappointed about Mrs F's disappearance, but she couldn't help

214

worrying. When she and Lily had time-travelled Mrs F had been close by and Lily wondered if that had helped in some way. Also she'd wanted to ask her about Rose Perkins, to check she would be ready as well. Oh well, I mustn't give up, she told herself. I must keep going with the plan. I can't leave Lily where she is and Aubrey's got to get home too.

At the top of St Michael's Hill she allowed herself a brief rest. The view of Bristol, set out before her, was so crystal clear, so beautiful, it took her breath away. The smoke- belching factories and stinking sewers had vanished. Instead there was clean, blue air and bright sunlight glancing off impossibly high glass towers . I'll never see this again, thought Rose. She tried to fix the image in her mind like a photograph, so she'd always remember it – just as it looked now. But she knew she couldn't stay long. She had to keep going, down the other side of the hill to the forbidding stone entrance of Bristol Children's Hospital.

'No unaccompanied children!' The bored-looking porter leaned forward and tapped his pen against the notice pinned to the front of his desk.' Sorry love.'

He didn't look at all sorry, or interested in Rose's pleading face. He just propped his newspaper up in front of him and carried on reading as though she wasn't there. Well, she thought to herself, I shan't be! Quietly, but purposefully she walked across the entrance hall and around the corner to the lifts. Once out of sight, she stopped and listened. Nothing! She couldn't believe it had been that easy. She went over to the lift button and pressed it confidently.

'Oi, where do you think you're off to?'

Rose swung around. But it wasn't the porter. It was a youngish man with light ginger hair. She recognised him from that early morning expedition down Chandos Road. He'd been standing in the doorway in his slippers and he'd reminded her of someone in her own time. Today he was dressed up in a white coat and checked trousers with a funny net hat on his head.

'Thought I recognised you. You live round my way, don't you?'

Rose nodded nervously. Was he going to throw her out? But as the doors pinged open he grinned and stepped aside to let her in.

'Which floor do you want then? I'm going down to the kitchens, so you press yours first.'

Lily pressed the third floor button and then looked hard at the metal wall in front of her, hoping he wouldn't ask her any more questions. But of course he did.

'Where's you Ma then? You're not here by yourself are you?'

'Oh no. Thank you for asking, but she's, um, er…' Rose thought desperately for something to say. 'She's already there – on the ward. Ward 17, I mean.'

The ginger guy looked down at her, his face suddenly very alert and interested: 'Isn't that the ward with the mystery boy on it? It was in the Evening Post – what a story! Do you know any more about it then?'

'No, nothing at all!' Rose was going hot with embarrassment at telling so many lies in such a short space of time. She breathed a sigh of relief as the doors rolled open and with a quick 'Good bye to you sir,' she jumped out. The last she saw of the ginger man was a puzzled face disappearing behind sliding doors, as the lift shot downwards.

She ran down the corridor then stopped, breathing heavily,

by the sign to Ward 17. I must walk in quickly and look really confident, she thought, just like I did downstairs. A couple of the nurses looked up as she strode up to Aubrey's door, but her purposeful manner must have fooled them – or else they were too busy to bother with a stray girl – and nobody tried to stop her. She turned the handle, the door swung open – the room was empty! Her heart sank. What now? The ward clock showed it was already five o'clock. She stared around her, no sign of the mystery boy. There was nothing for it, she'd have to ask someone, so she marched up to one of the nurses.

'Where's Aub... I mean, where's the boy from *that* room?' Rose jabbed her thumb towards Aubrey's door.

The nurse was bending over a little girl who was covered in a strange orange rash. She glanced up at Rose.

'He's in the TV lounge, I think.' She paused and looked quizzically at Rose. 'You've visited him before haven't you?'

'Oh yes,' Rose thought quickly. 'Dr Steele arranged it to cheer him up 'cos he hasn't any family to come in.'

'Okay.' The nurse seemed satisfied with this. 'First door on your right, it's got 'TV Lounge' written on it – you can't miss it.'

She went back to examining the rash and Rose set off down the ward. It was easy enough to find the room. *Please* let Aubrey be in here, Rose prayed as she pushed open the door. It was small, stuffy and very dark in there. Five or six children were huddled around the screen with their backs to her but she could pick out Aubrey straight away from his dark hair and the pale skin of his neck. He swivelled round as she came in and Rose had to stop herself laughing out loud. Someone must have lent him some clothes. He was wearing a hooded sweatshirt and jeans, topped off with a baseball cap worn backwards. It just didn't look right. After all Rose was used to seeing him brown knickerbockers and an Eton jacket. Rose went over and tugged at his arm.

'We're going. Right now!' she hissed dramatically. 'Don't ask questions, just come with me. It's really important.'

Aubrey looked round longingly at the TV. 'Can't we just stay a bit longer? The programme's nearly finished.'

'No!'

Rose's expression was so fierce that Aubrey didn't ask again, but jumped up and followed her quickly out into the corridor.

'Now,' Rose hissed. 'Look like you know exactly where you're going. Don't stop or look round and if I say the word run for your life!'

'My, you've got awfully bossy in your old age...' Aubrey stopped abruptly, silenced by a thunderous look from Rose. 'Alright old chum, anything you say. Sally forth!'

They got back to the lift, but there were too many people waiting and Rose didn't want to get caught up in any more awkward conversations, so she looked around for the stairs. She spotted them just to the left of the lift doors and beckoned at Aubrey to follow her. Silently they sped down to the entrance level. Luckily it was full of people milling around and she and Aubrey managed to attach themselves to a large, noisy family who were making for the door. Rose reached over and pulled Aubrey's hat down over his face as they went past the doorman. She didn't want anyone raising the alarm just yet.

As they hit the street, Aubrey stopped dead in his tracks.'

Whew, look at all those motors!'

'No time to stare Aubrey. We've got to get back to Brighton Street before Sylvia gets back.'

'Brighton Street? Why are we going there? What's happened to Cossins Place? And who's Sylvia?'

'I can't explain now. Cossins Place is still there, but Brighton Street is where I live now, and so does your Dr Steele. It's all different from what we're used to. I'll tell you more when we get back – oh my goodness!'

'What's up, Rose?'

'Have you got the crystal? It's like a piece of glass – I think Mrs F gave it to you…'

Aubrey looked surprised and then grinned. 'Calm down, old girl! Of course I have. The nurses tried to take it away – to disinfect it or something – but I managed to keep it out of their grasp. Hey, how did you know about it?'

Rose breathed a sigh of relief – she hadn't fancied dodging the hospital porters again.

'Don't ask any more questions. I'll explain everything once we're back – come on!'

They got back to Brighton Street with just five minutes to spare. Please, please don't let Sylvia be early, Rose prayed. But she needn't have worried. Sylvia was never early for anything and came puffing in, with overflowing bags, almost twenty minutes later.

'So sorry, darling. Everything okay?'

'Yes, thank you for asking.' Rose smiled up at her, safe in the knowledge that Aubrey was tucked up in Lily's wardrobe with some biscuits and a stack of comics.

'Well, I've had a good day, sold the lot! And I've bought some fantastic organic wool from the Shetlands, so I can get going on those ponchos. You'll be able to help me with all your local knowledge from Peru!'

Rose gulped, but Sylvia continued merrily on, 'It's a good omen, Rose. I'm sure we'll hear from Mark and Lily soon. Do you know, it's an odd thing, but I saw the old lady from the wool shop at the fair. She's a funny old stick, but I've always rather liked her, such kind eyes.'

'What did she say? I mean did she tell you anything?' Rose could hardly contain her excitement, but Sylvia continued dreamily scrubbing carrots in the sink and humming to herself. Rose went over and tugged at her cardigan. She would never normally have done this to an adult, but she had to get Sylvia's attention.

'Please, Sylvia, try and remember! What did Mrs F say to you?'

Sylvia looked down at her with surprise. 'Sorry, Rose, I was miles away. You want to know what she said? Well you know what she's like. She tends to ramble on a bit and I was trying to pack up the stall before it rained...' She glanced over at Rose, who was hopping up and down with anticipation. 'Oh dear, I'm trying to think. It was something like 'All will be well'. That's a quote from somewhere – a poem or a prayer by Julian of Norwich I think. She was a Nun, a mystic, in medieval times...'

'Was that all she said?' Rose interrupted rudely.

Sylvia creased up her forehead. 'Well the rest was just about the weather. I honestly don't think it was important.'

Rose turned away disappointedly. She'd been hoping for

something more, some instructions for instance on how to get everyone back safely. It was all very well for Mrs F to say 'All will be well', but how could she be so sure? Rose didn't feel sure at all.

'Rose, darling, I almost forgot the best news of all!' Sylvia fished around in one of the deep pockets of her cardigan and waved a bulky envelope at her. 'Air tickets!' She beamed over at Rose.' You're going home!

CHAPTER TWENTY ONE
All Will Be Well

'Dear Sylvia,

I'm sorry I haven't written for a while, but the postal service here is a nightmare! I'm so much better now and missing Rose like mad. The house is far too quiet – and far too tidy – without her! So I'm ready to have her back, if that's okay with you and Lily. What a lovely time they must have had. Maybe one day Lily could come and visit us out here? I enclose the tickets for the return journey. I hope they get to you in time – it's rather short notice, but as you know we still have no phones in the village!

Thank you again. A million thank you's! You know I would do the same for you if you ever needed me to.

Lots of love

Your best friend, Caroline

Rose re-read it for the hundredth time and held the thick card of the tickets in her hand, checking and re-checking the date.

The 18th of June – tomorrow! If she couldn't travel back in time tonight, she would be put on a plane to Peru in the morning. And if she went to Peru, Aubrey would have to get back by himself and the real Rose Perkins would be stuck in the past forever. She told Sylvia she was going upstairs to pack and carefully opened up the door to the wardrobe.

Aubrey was sitting inside looking very cosy, surrounded by piles of comics and biscuit wrappers.

'Hullo, old bean! What's up?' he looked anxiously at Rose's worried face.

She put her finger to her lips. 'Shh. You've got to be really quiet in case Sylvia hears and comes upstairs!'

In the half light of the wardrobe, Aubrey's face glowed deathly white, his dark eyes almost disappearing into the darkness.

'What are we going to do?' he mouthed at her.

Rose crumpled the letter in her hand. She was tired of making all the decisions and being responsible for everything. 'I don't know,' she said flatly.

'Well at least tell me what's going on. All I know is I got really sick and they came to take me to the fever hospital, but on my way there everything went really woozy and the next thing I know I'm lying under a tree in the park. Then I'm carted off to that weird hospital with all the machines and people in funny clothes.'

'You're in the future. It's 2008. I know it sounds crazy, but it's true,' Rose could see Aubrey's disbelieving expression even in the gloom of the wardrobe. 'Look why don't I tell you from the beginning. Do you remember the day we rollerskated in the park?'

***

'And that's as much as I know.' Rose eased her legs out from underneath her. They were cramped and full of pins and needles from kneeling on them too long. Aubrey frowned back at her.

'It's not much is it? I mean there's loads you don't know, isn't there?'

'I thought I explained it very well,' answered Rose huffily. '*And* I think you'll find we saved your life, so don't complain too much!'

'I wasn't complaining, silly! I was just saying there are still lots of unanswered questions – like how do we get back? You say you came here from 12 Cossins Place and I went to Cotham Park from Number 46, and we don't know exactly where Rose Perkins and Lily went. But Lily must have been near enough to the park to leave her note under the tree. So it looks as though all the time-travelling happens either on, or very close, to Cossins Place…I say have you got a map? I've got an idea!'

Rose ran downstairs to the kitchen, where Sylvia was stirring a pot of vegetables. 'Mrs Sta – I mean Sylvia – could I take a map of Redland back with me, as a reminder of my visit? Please – I'd really like to show my mother when I get back.'

'Alright, sweetie. Actually she'd love that because we shared a flat here when we were students, right above the wool shop on Chandos Road.' She stopped, seeing Rose's astonished expression. 'Yes, darling, that's how I know Mrs F and that's how I got into the knitting. Oh, me and your mum had such good times in that flat! I'm fairly sure it was at one of our parties there that she met your Dad – it all seems just like yesterday…' Sylvia tailed off dreamily. 'Oh goodness! You're after a map aren't you? There's a small one in the wicker basket over by the washing machine. Yes that's the one. I've nearly finished here and then I'll be up to help you pack, alright?'

'Yes, of course. Thank you very much, Sylvia.'

Rose raced back up to Lily's room.

'Quick! We haven't much time, Sylvia's on her way up. Show me what you mean.' Rose thrust the map down in front of the wardrobe and Aubrey stared at it for a few minutes before making some marks against their house numbers and the park.

'Bring me a ruler. I want to try something.'

Rose fetched him one. Aubrey paused thoughtfully, and then placed the ruler on the map and swiftly drew five lines. He looked up at Rose, 'What does that look like to you?'

Rose stared down at the page. It was very clear what it was. 'It's a pentangle; it looks exactly like the one above the wool shop. Cook used to say it was a sign of witchcraft, but Janetta said it was a much older magic than that.'

Aubrey stared up at her, his eyes glittering. 'Now. Look for the centre of the pentangle.'

Rose studied it for a few seconds. 'Why it's right on the wool shop, on Chandos Road! Aubrey…'

'So I reckon,' continued Aubrey breathlessly, 'that if we're anywhere inside the pentangle we can travel back in time.'

'And the crystal!' exclaimed Rose. 'You have to have a piece of Mrs F's crystal ball to wish. I don't think it works unless you hold it.'

Aubrey nodded. 'She gave it to me the day you and I went rollerskating. I had to get some buttons for Ma and the old bat in the wool shop went all peculiar on me, said I was in 'Great Danger'! I thought it was all rot at the time, but it turns out she was right…' Aubrey stopped and gave Rose a searching look. 'Who is she Rose? And why did she choose to save *us*?'

'I don't know, and perhaps we never will. She's gone away. She's sold the shop and gone off travelling in her tent somewhere. Sylvia saw her today at the fair and Mrs F told her 'All will be well'. Maybe it will be…'

'We still need a plan for tonight, though,' pointed out Aubrey.' We've all four got to be in the pentagon *and* holding our crystals *and* wishing at the same time. What's up?'

Rose was looking thoughtful. 'I was thinking about the first time I time-travelled. I was wishing really hard because I was so afraid of dying of diphtheria. But why was Rose Perkins wishing? It's so lovely here, I wouldn't have wanted to leave!'

'Yes, but she didn't know it was going to be lovely,' reasoned Aubrey. 'She'd lived in that little village in Peru all her life *and* her mum was very ill. Maybe she was really scared. What's more important point is, how can we be sure she knows to wish tonight? Do you think Lily might have told her?'

Rose shook her head. 'She didn't mention it in her note. But if Lily hasn't told her, I think Mrs F will have. She did say 'All will be well' and we know she can move around in time. I do wonder how Rose Perkins got *her* piece of the crystal though…?'

But even as Rose asked the question she realised she already knew the answer. 'Of course! Her mum lived above the wool shop. Mrs F must have given it to Caroline then – and she must have passed it on to Rose.'

Aubrey crinkled up his forehead. 'That would mean the old lady's been planning all this for a very long time.'

'I don't think time works in quite the same way for Mrs F as it does for us… ' Rose stiffened suddenly. 'Sylvia's coming up stairs! Quick, shut the door and try not to move. Or breathe!'

'I can't not breathe you idiot…' But Aubrey's protests were cut short by Rose slamming the door shut, just as Sylvia marched in.

When Sylvia bent to kiss her goodnight Rose put her arms up and gave her a long tight hug. 'Thank you Sylvia. Thank you so much for everything. I'll never forget you and Lily. When you see Lily give her a big hug from me and tell her she's been my best friend and I'll always remember her. For as long as I live!'

'Yes of course, darling, of course I will. But I'll see you tomorrow. I'm taking you to the airport first thing in the morning, so we can say goodbye properly then.'

Even so, Sylvia's voice was shaky and Rose could see the tears welling up in her eyes. Rose longed to tell her the truth: that she never would see her again, that the little girl she drove to the airport tomorrow would, if everything worked out, be a stranger. But she didn't dare risk it. You never could be sure how adults would react to things and she mustn't put their plan in danger now. They were so nearly there, a few more hours and everyone would be on their way home.

As soon as Sylvia's footsteps had faded down the stairs, Rose slipped out of bed. She took a piece of paper, wrote quickly on it and placed it under Lily's pillow. Then she tip-toed over to the wardrobe. 'Aubrey, are you there? Are you ready?'

Aubrey pushed the doors open. The hinges made a loud creaking noise and for a few moments they both held their breath. But there was no sound from below and Aubrey stepped out of the wardrobe, rubbing his cramped limbs.

'Phew! I'm glad to be out of that hole. My legs had gone to sleep and there's a limit to how long a chap can hold his breath!' He gave Rose a mischievous smile.

Rose grinned back at him and felt a sudden rush of happiness and relief. Relief that he hadn't died and happy that they had saved his life, that he could be here now, smiling, in Lily's bedroom, not dying in a Victorian fever hospital.

'So what now? When do we wish?' Aubrey looked expectantly at her.

Rose frowned. 'Mrs F didn't give me any clues about that. And the other thing is, how will Lily and Rose Perkins know when the right time is? We should all wish together. Oh, the more I try and work it out the more frazzled my brain gets!'

Aubrey leaned over and took her hand. Just for a moment Rose wondered if he was going to kiss her again. But he didn't. Instead he turned her wrist over and looked down at her watch.

'Ten o'clock. You know if I was Lily – or Rose Perkins – and I knew I had to wish at a certain time and I had to guess what that time was – I know what I'd guess.'

Rose nodded, she realised she knew it too. 'Midnight, of course.'

Aubrey grinned. 'So we might as well settle down for the next couple of hours, then at the stroke of twelve we'll both wish together. I'm sure it's going to work. I just know it. In two hours I'll be back with Ma and Father – and the little brats – and you'll be safely tucked up in bed at number 12… I say Rose what's the matter?' He was looking at Rose's pinched, white face. 'You do *want* to go back, don't you Rose?'

Rose didn't reply. It was a question she'd been trying not to ask herself because it had an answer she didn't want to think about. 'Back' meant her mother's angry silences and endless tellings off. 'Back' meant no school, no friends. 'Back' meant nothing to look forward to except long sermons and dull walks in the park. Did she really want to give up everything she had here, for that?

After all, she *could* stay. She didn't *have* to wish when the others did. Aubrey wouldn't know until it was too late and he was back in his own time. She'd fooled Sylvia into thinking she was Rose Perkins, so she must look very like her. Perhaps she could fool Caroline too? She could get on that plane tomorrow and live the rest of her life in this modern world, with its TVs and marvellous medicines and clean, bright air. There'd be nobody telling her how sinful she was and making her feel guilty all the time. No stiff boots and annoying hats. No gristly lumps of meat and over-boiled cabbage. If she stayed here she could go to school and university. She could become Prime Minister and even fly to the moon if she wanted to! So *why*? Why on earth would she want to give all this up and go back to her own time?

'Hey, Rose, I was only joking. I didn't mean it seriously.' Aubrey was looking at her with an alarmed expression on his face.

'You *have* to come back, it would be wicked to leave Rose Perkins there – and anyway I think it would be wrong, in some way, for time itself. I can't explain it properly, but we've meddled with time and now we've got to put it right again.'

Rose didn't answer straight away. She was staring out of the darkening window. After a long pause she spoke, 'Well, what are we going to do until midnight then?'

Aubrey smiled, relieved. 'You're going to tell me everything. Everything you've seen and done here in the future. I want to know all about the machines I saw on the TV – the cars and the aeroplanes – and have there really been spaceships to the moon? Everything!

So they talked. Rose leant back against the pillows on her bed. Aubrey crouched on the floor, his back against the wardrobe in case he needed to hide again quickly. Time seemed to pass both very slowly and very fast. They never ran out of things to say to one another and the minutes and hours slipped away, until Aubrey leaned forward and grabbed Rose's wrist again. 'Two minutes to twelve. Phew Rose. We nearly missed it!'

Rose stared down at her watch. The short hand was on the twelve and the minute hand was nudging closer and closer to it.

She looked up at Aubrey, her eyes wide with fear and excitement. 'Now, Aubrey! Wish now!'

Epilogue

'Rose! Rose! The car's running outside, bring your case down. We'd better be off now, or we'll miss the plane!'

Lily lay in bed hardly daring to open her eyes. Was she dreaming? Was that really her mum's voice? And was that the radio she could hear and the hum of cars driving up and down the street? She opened her eyes. There was an explosion of pinks and yellows and blues. A huge wave of relief poured over her, as she took in the piles of clothes and toys strewn over the floor. Her bedroom! Her own bedroom at home. She was back in her own time!

She sat up and turned to look out of the window. Then a thump of fear hit her. A girl was standing there, silhouetted against the glass. A girl with long dark hair. A girl who looked like Rose, but wasn't Rose at all. Then the girl smiled.

'Hello, Lily. I'm glad we've met at last.'

Lily stared back at her, her mind whirling with questions. 'Who are you? What are you doing in my bedroom? Where's the real Rose?'

The girl continued smiling patiently at her. 'I *am* the real Rose and I've been… sort of travelling. And today I woke up here, which is actually where I started from. Does any of this make any sense to you?'

Lily screwed up her face with the effort of trying to sort it all out. 'I... I think so. Are you Rose Perkins? Are you from Peru?'

The girl nodded and had just opened her mouth to speak again when they heard the front door bang and Sylvia's voice shouting up.

'Are you alright, sweetie? Do you need a hand with your suitcase?'

The girl turned and picked up her bag. 'Coming, Sylvia!'

As she reached the door Lily blurted out. 'What was it like for you? Was it alright?'

Rose Perkins grinned back at her. 'It was brilliant!'

Then she was gone. The front door slammed and the car revved off down the street. Lily rocked back in her bed, hugging her knees to her chest. She had a few hours now to plan what she would tell her mum. She would say that she'd had a good time with her dad but she didn't want to live with him in America. With any luck Sylvia would be so relieved to see her she wouldn't press her for too much information. And meanwhile she was so glad, *so glad*, to be back in the 21st century!

One morning, a few weeks later, a blue air mail letter dropped through the door. It was from Mark. He'd decided to sell his house and set up a new business in Australia and so, he was really sorry, but he was going to be too busy to have Lily just at the moment. He'd be in touch... Sylvia sighed and shook her head.

'Honestly, after all that fuss about custody and now look! He's flitting off again.' She smiled warmly across the breakfast table at Lily. 'Well, at least that's a weight off *my* mind. Looks like it's just the two of us again, darling.'

***

At first Lily was so relieved to be back in her own time that she hardly gave a thought to how Rose and Aubrey – or Frances and Edie – might be getting on. Yes, she missed Rose's company, but things were so much better at school now. Even though Rose was gone, the other girls still included Lily in all their games, and there were no more lonely break times. Her teachers seemed amazingly relaxed and friendly after the horrors of the Axteds Establishment for Young Ladies. And Miss Wright said her hand writing had improved enormously!

Another week passed and another blue airmail letter appeared on the mat. This time it was addressed to Lily and when she tore it open a photograph fell out. It showed a thin, dark-haired girl in shorts – the same girl who had appeared in her bedroom the morning Lily had travelled back in time.

Sylvia peered over her shoulder. 'Oh what a lovely picture of Rose! She looks very grown up, doesn't she? I'm glad she's alright. She seemed a little peaky when I saw her off, not quite herself somehow…'

Lily stared hard at the photo. If she looked at it from a certain angle it did seem like Rose – *her* Rose – but when she tilted it another way, a stranger looked back at her. The girl wasn't facing directly at the camera, but slightly off to the edge of the photo and she had a strange, secret smile on her lips. Her hands were curled in her lap, one of them more loosely open than the other. And in that hand Lily could make out the outline of a jagged object. She brought the picture right up close to her eyes, but the image remained blurry and unclear. It's the crystal, thought Lily. I bet you anything that's her piece of the crystal ball.

She smoothed out the letter and started to read:

Dear Lily,

Thank you so much for the amazing time I had in England. I'll never forget our adventures there. Mum keeps asking me about school and friends and stuff. I keep telling her there was so much going on I can't possibly remember it all, but perhaps you could remind me of a few things, names of teachers, places we visited – you know what I mean!

I hope we'll meet again one day. Mrs F said we might. You do know Mrs F, don't you?

Lots of love Rose xxxxx

Lily smiled to herself. She knew exactly what Rose meant. She wrote off a letter at once with all the details Rose might need to fill in the weeks she should have spent with them in Redland. A month passed. Lily's life returned pretty much to normal: home, school, home, play, bed.

One day, on her way to school, Dr Steele cycled past. When he saw Lily he screeched to a halt and pulled his bike up to tell her, 'Thought you'd like to know about the mystery boy Lily. Seems he recovered completely from the diphtheria and they were just about to take him off to a children's home when he disappeared into thin air! Don't suppose you know anything about that do you Lily?'

Lily's heart missed a beat. How much did he know about Rose and Aubrey? Had the grownups suspected something after all? Then she looked up and saw to her relief that he was grinning at her.

'You'll have to write off to Rose and ask her,' he went on. 'She's the one with the special powers isn't she?' And still chuckling to himself he threw his leg over his saddle and peddled madly off down Chandos Road.

Freddy had got a lot more annoying since she'd got back. He'd started hanging around, staring intently at her and asking loads of questions about Rose. He made it sound like he and Rose had spent a quite a bit of time together, which Lily found hard to believe.

'Did Rose tell you about the secret box?'

They were on their way back from school and Freddy was walking so close to Lily he kept bumping her with his football bag.

'No – and stop walloping me with your kit. Those boots are really hard!'

'Sorry,' said Freddy, in uncharacteristically polite mode. 'But are you sure she didn't say anything to you?'

'Nope.' Lily was trying to work out if she had enough money for a comic and sweets.

'Nothing about a box? Under a tree? In the park?'

Lily stopped dead, then swung around to face him. 'What did she tell you?' She must have looked really fierce, because Freddy backed away looking alarmed.

'Whoa! So you *do* know about it. Why's it such a big secret then? Why did you pretend not to know about it?'

'I wasn't pretending – I just wasn't listening properly.' Lily paused, wondering how much Freddy knew. 'So how did you find the box, Freddy?'

'I didn't, Rose did.' Freddy told Lily what had happened that day in the park. 'And she took it home with her, even though I'd shown her it was empty. I kept asking her why she was bothering with an old tin and she said it was like a time capsule and I wouldn't understand, which was a bit rude of her. Hey! I've got an idea lets go and see if there are any more buried there.'

Lily knew, of course, that there wouldn't be any more boxes under the tree. But she couldn't think of anything better to do, so they made their way – after an essential stop at the sweet shop – over to the park. As they passed Number 48 Cossins Place, Lily looked up at the blank windows and gave a shiver. An image of Edie with her white nightgown and pleading eyes flashed into her mind. Oh, Edie I hope you got away, she thought to herself. I hope you got that big house in the country and all those children with their party dresses and pink buns!

Lily ran ahead, not stopping until she came under the broad, green tent of the oak's branches. She stared up at the huge tree. Only a few days ago she'd stood here with Edie and Frances and it had been just a tiny sapling, barely reaching her knees.

Freddy ambled up to her, a lollipop jammed in one side of his mouth. 'I've found a good stone to dig with. I'll start and you can watch.' He stopped, seeing Lily's disgusted expression. 'And then we'll swap over. I did find the stone!' He knelt down and started scraping away around the roots of the tree. 'Urff! It's really hard work digging round these things and there's tons of stones. I'll see if I can go any deeper... hang on a minute! What's this?' His stone was chinking against something metal. 'It's right inside the roots – must have been here for years...' He dug deeper and loosened the earth around a rectangular grey box. 'Here we go!' grunted Freddy triumphantly, as he finally pulled it free and flipped open the lid. His face turned ashen as he stared into the box. Slowly he turned round to face Lily, his voice trembling as he spoke, 'There's an envelope in here – and it's addressed to you!'

This time Freddy didn't try to grab the box. Instead, he thrust it quickly into Lily's hands. He looked pale and shaky.

'There's something going on isn't there? Something a bit spooky, something to do with you and that Rose girl?'

Lily bit her lip and stared at the scuffed-up grass beneath the tree. She was tired, really tired, of all the secrets and lies.

'I can't tell you everything. I really can't. I'm not just being mean. But you are right, there has been something strange going on.'

Freddy gazed at her, his face perfectly serious. 'It's to do with time isn't it? You've kind of half told me that already.'

'Yes, it is to do with time. Oh, Freddy, I really can't say anymore! It wouldn't be right. Something good happened. We *actually* saved someone's life, and I'm afraid if I told you the truth about it, it would all be undone. And it was quite hard to do it actually. It wasn't easy and I don't think I could manage it again…' Lily realised she was going to cry and fiercely blinked back the tears. But this time Freddy didn't tease or laugh at her. He shoved his hands deep into his pockets and stared into the far distance beyond the railway line.

'Okay, I won't ask what's in the letter, or any more about the time thing. If it's really that important you can keep it a secret. Come on! Let's go home.'

Lily cradled the precious envelope in her hands, all the way back to Brighton Street. As soon as they got to the Steele's house

Freddy vaulted over the low garden wall and with a brief 'See ya!' he was gone.

Lily sat on the steps of her house, the last rays of the evening sun warming her bare arms. Then she opened the letter.

Dear Lily,

Are you still eleven? Well, I have a shock for you – I am eighty years old! It's the summer of 1968. I don't often get to visit Bristol these days, I've lived abroad for such a long time now. Do you remember how I so wanted to travel and see the world? Well I did! But I'm getting ahead of myself. You'll want to know what happened when I got back to my own time. It took all my courage to wish to go back . I so nearly didn't, and then I would have gone off to Peru instead of Rose Perkins and that would have been a whole other story. But of course it was the right thing to do and now I'm so glad I went home. I was a different girl when I got back – everybody said so – and in my mother's opinion it definitely wasn't an improvement! I insisted I went to school and spent many happy years at the new Redland High School. It was such a relief to have lessons with other girls and I loved playing hockey on the Downs. It felt wonderful after those awful struggles with Mama! I do hope your school works out well for you in the end – really you don't know how lucky you are.

Now for some sad news: I know you'll want to know about Aubrey, how we used to meet up in the park after school, how I finally got the hang of roller-skating! How we kept in touch after he was posted to India, how we planned to get married as soon as he'd made enough money for me to come over and join him.

Then the Great War started. Aubrey was one of the first to volunteer. He was killed in August 1916. Now, I don't want you to feel sorry for me. I've had a wonderful life. Do you remember Neville? Aubrey's younger brother, with the flame-red hair? Well, we married after the war and because of his job as a diplomat we lived all over the world and had two wonderful sons. We also have some lovely grandchildren, one of them is a little girl called Caroline. Sadly her parents are divorced but I know she spends a lot of time with her best friend Sylvia and her family. Yes, I know, we never guessed who Rose Perkins was did we? She was my own great granddaughter!

Now, I know you'll be wondering: what was the point of rescuing Aubrey, when he was only going to be killed in the war a few years later? Well it was this. He was the love of my life. It was worth every minute of every day I spent with him.

So thank you, Lily, for being a part of it, and being so brave and taking that step into the unknown, just because I asked you to. Thank you, Lily.
All my love, for ever,
Rose

Lightning Source UK Ltd.
Milton Keynes UK
15 December 2010

164434UK00001B/30/P